# City of Death

# City of Death

Abheek Barua

juggernaut

JUGGERNAUT BOOKS
KS House, 118 Shahpur Jat, New Delhi 110049, India

First published by Juggernaut Books 2016



ISBN 9788193237212

Typeset in Adobe Caslon Pro by R. Ajith Kumar, New Delhi

Printed at Manipal Technologies Ltd

# City of Death

# 1

# The Killing

She is propped up against the wall, her hands and feet bound, a tight gag almost choking her. Her eyes are open and in them he reads a combination of disbelief and terror. The smell that assails his nostrils tells him that her sphincter muscle has refused to hold on to the last vestige of human dignity and she has shat herself copiously.

He has just returned from the bathroom and is naked. His body is waxed and hairless; the shock of dense, curly pubic hair is in startling contrast to it. In his right hand he carries a cleaver of the kind that butchers use to chop mutton on their wooden blocks. Both his hands are sheathed in cheap latex surgical gloves and he wears both a hairnet and improvised polythene socks that make him look slightly comical. The initial exhilaration and the anxiety at the sheer audacity of his act have subsided and he feels the slow transformation into a calmer, self-possessed, rational self.

There is an almost inaudible mewling coming from behind the gag. Is she entreating him to spare her so that she can return to the life that she has professed to so hate? Why can't she realize that this is an act of mercy that he is offering her? A word learnt in an afternoon divinity class endured decades ago comes back to him – benediction. This is how he will bless her, this will be his benediction. He feels ordained, god's licensed messenger for the next few minutes.

He knows from her long conversations with him that every waking moment of her day she is tormented by guilt. She has not found the means to atone. At barely twenty-three she has been left bereft of the pleasures of the body that are so essential to the act of living. The first hint of foreplay makes her flinch, her legs instead of splaying open clamp shut, she parches instead of secreting, a combined reflex to stave off penetration. Intercourse forced on her a few times has invariably led to self-harm – cuts to her arms or her thighs with a knife or a blade, wrought with almost religious fervour.

But this is not merely an act of compassion. He is here for himself as well. Experts have described his killings in the past as an appeasement of a deity whose ire he has invoked – the classic black box of sacrifice as propitiation. He cannot suppress a smile when he thinks how wrong they were.

He had stopped caring about rituals when he was a child

of six or seven. The rhythmic chanting from the canons of his religion did not soothe him, nor did the exhortations to find peace within himself take away the torment. He has spent hours in meditative reflection but he has tired of the passivity of this process.

His spiritual path is more active – the breaking down of all that society decrees as taboo. He has trained his body and mind not to discriminate between the clean and the defiled, the living and the dead, the supposedly sacred and the profane. He knows that he is not alone in this; a shadowy, forbidding corner of his religion has for centuries offered this path to seekers.

But now, yet again, he needs to take the next step. The final step – the taking of another life without bearing either hatred or compassion or the smallest drop of guilt. He moves forward, grabs her by the hair, steadies her head and raises the cleaver. The mewling rises to a crescendo but he is certain it cannot be heard outside with all the windows in the room tightly shut and the air conditioner humming. There are no mantras to be chanted now, no passion to be felt. As the cleaver swings towards her fair, slender neck his eyes are fixed on the target and curiously devoid of all emotion.

He has never thought of freeing himself from the eternal cycle of birth, death and rebirth. That is all too abstract for him. However, he believes in the possible and this is a philosophy that is entirely his own. There is a pastiche of ideas, of events and influences that have left their imprint.

He takes pride in that he, the lone individual, has shaped them into a system of belief that culminates in this action. He is not a preacher, wants no followers and is perfectly content in the fact that he is the sole audience of his sermon. In this brief life he wants to rise above the banalities and pettiness, the meaningless rhythms that define the act of living. He has always wanted to transcend. With this kill, he has transcended again.

The severed carotid has sprayed his body with blood like a fireman's hose that has spun out of control. He walks into the bathroom, has a long shower alternating between scalding hot and freezing cold, using the soap he has carried with him. He dries himself, stuffs the gloves, hairnet and socks into a polythene bag, wears his clothes with a degree of care, and finally the shoes that he has taken off at the door. He walks towards the window and peers out to see if there is anyone outside. It is eleven at night, it's drizzling and the streets are quiet and empty. The street lamps barely shed any light. He gently opens the door with a handkerchief covering his hand, walks down the small concrete path, unlatches the small iron gate and steps on to the pavement with his small travel case.

He will walk a mile or so before he hails a cab and goes home. He is hungry and his stomach is growling. It's time for dinner.

# 2

# Sohini Sen

The living room is always dark with the drapes blocking the slimmest shard of even the brightest afternoon sun. They are, however, the second line of defence against the invasion of light. The house was renovated a couple of years ago but has resisted the tyranny of glass that the new builders have imposed on this sun-surfeit city. The wooden shutters remain with their adjustable louvres that are closed shut. It is afternoon and she slouches in her well-worn burgundy armchair. An old cassette, testimony to her aversion to technological change, plays on an equally old boom box. The music is a Rachmaninoff piano sonata – its wintery Russian bleakness marks a sharp contrast to the hot stuffiness of the room.

She is just back from work and feels the onset of a dull headache. The mix of the two pills that she has popped in the morning and the large shot of Smirnoff vodka to wash them down have brought this on. Usually they induce a slow creeping somnolence around noon. The chemistry of the two is, however, difficult to predict and these headaches, though not frequent, are not rare either.

As has been her practice for the past year, she has left the office around one in the afternoon. Her colleagues do not expect her to return. She has dispensed with the tedious fabrication of excuses – the urgent meetings, crises at home – and her personal assistant, Mullick, knows better than to ask her if she will be back in her slightly oversized swivel chair later in the day. Before she leaves in the morning she makes every effort to mask the reek of alcohol, brushing her teeth vigorously and chewing mints. However, the fact that she cannot face the day without her morning tipple and her psychotropic helpers is clear for everyone to see. The slight slurring of her speech, the sourness of breath that overpowers the mint and toothpaste, and the small but frequent lapses of short-term memory give her away.

'Have you booked your ticket for Goa?' her mother asks from her bedroom where she usually spends her afternoons lying on her bed and reading old issues of the *Economist* borrowed from the British Council library and occasionally a tattered, antique *Punch*.

'Yes, I did this morning,' she lies, cursing herself for forgetting yet again to get on the airline site and get herself the cheapest flight for the following Saturday morning when

Sajal will pick her up from Dabolim airport.

Sajal is staying for a year in a small artist's residency in south Goa funded by one of the state's mining barons. He is a middle-tier artist who after a degree in political science went through the entire rigmarole of art school. Sajal was her classmate through both school and college. He was quite unabashedly infatuated with her though his clumsy efforts to convey his emotions went largely unrequited. Her romantic interest lay elsewhere, in gaunt and bespectacled Orko, reciting from heart both morbid Sylvia Plath and the enigmatic Jibanananda Das with equal ease and passion – the quintessential high school and college poseur. He was now a rotund fund manager in California, married to an American, father of two athletic kids and his only link to India was the periodic company visits he made to sniff out profits for his portfolio.

Despite his romantic disappointment, Sajal remains the only friend from school who has kept in touch with her. 'You must visit me here,' he had pleaded. 'South Goa is very different. None of that water sports crap. The residency is right on a beach that's almost private. They have plenty of spare rooms and they don't mind my having a guest over.'

She had acquiesced but not because she craved Sajal's company. In fact, she found him mildly annoying – all that silly reminiscing about school and college, all the bits and bytes of information about long-lost school friends mined from Facebook pages, their children with their myriad achievements ('...and Oindrila, Rakhee's daughter, has got into the National Institute of Design') and photo updates of their parties featuring tables laden with food and men holding whisky glasses, forced smiles on their ageing faces. She would be in Goa next week because it fitted into her plan.

She felt a twinge of sympathy for him. Poor Sajal, who she had twirled around her fingers all her life – forcing him to spend his pocket money on pages of superhero stickers when they were in second grade, making him stand patiently in queue to collect her photocopies at the tiny Xerox shop at the corner of the college grounds while she gabbed with Orko in the canteen – she could compile an endless list of favours. This would be her final act of selfish exploitation of her friend. She felt a sense of relief that she would have no need left or the opportunity to atone.

Her plan for Goa is to wake up one morning at the crack of dawn. She would then walk into the sea, slowly first and then with an increasing sense of urgency until the waves grabbed her and took her away from the endlessness that was her life. She remembers the scene from *The Hours* where Nicole Kidman, playing Virginia Woolf with a crooked nose that a clever make-up artist had affixed, walks into the river to drown. She must remember, like the celluloid Woolf, to fill the pockets of her nightgown with stones to ensure that the sheer force of physics thwarts the human body's indomitable urge to survive. That and a few pills, all washed down with generous amounts of liquor, should, she believes, do the trick.

She could have killed herself here. That would save Sajal from hours of grilling by the Goa police, answering humiliating questions about the nature of their relationship ('No sex? Just a friend. Are you sure?') while the policemen sniggered and traded jokes in Konkani. She has been told that the sea has a habit of returning the remains of her kill to the land. Bodies don't float away like a message-bearing bottle, they wash up on the shore. If that was true, Sajal would have to face the gut-wrenching task of fetching the body from the morgue after the forensic doctors had finished with their post-mortem and then informing her mother. But Sajal, she thinks in a sudden lapse into cruelty, was always meant to be exploited.

She has chosen Goa instead as she does not want to die in this city. She wants to spend her last moments away from the stench of garbage, the sewers in the impossibly narrow lanes overflowing with the piss of squatting men, the blaring horns of cars careening down the rutted streets and the peeling paint of the rain-drenched houses covered with dirty green moss clumped together in a medieval disregard for the principles of modern planning. She wants to die in a pretty place, picture-postcard pretty.

Besides she has no attachments left here – no one to call for a Sunday morning banter or have the occasional cup of coffee with. Her friends have all left the city in search of work, a better life, a sense of freedom. In fact, her entire generation has left, their daily connect to their homeland a mash of liberal heart bleed and diligent 'likes' on crowded social media pages, returning once a year during the more bearable winter months, huddling together in the city's old colonial clubs, guzzling beer and kebabs, smug in their faraway lives, their old lives in the city a fading memory they are afraid to jettison altogether.

Her father, a student historian with a deep interest in the First World War, had told her about how the muddy trenches of the Somme and Ypres had swallowed up an entire generation of Europeans during the first war, leaving only the old, the infirm and the tender. She often feels that this city is similar. No able bodies, just a swarm of dependants getting by with no one to depend on.

---

Sohini Sen, Class of 1989, Economics, in one of the city's best-known colleges, the bulwark of two hundred years of academic distinction holding up the crumbling yellow buildings, had chosen not to join the legions of students who had migrated to the American Ivy league to write a doctoral thesis and join the exhausting battle for tenure. Economics as a subject left her cold. The tediousness of the complex proofs of mock theorems that pretend to mimic human behaviour and the sheer disdain for the application of what passed off as 'high theory' to any genuine human problem was not something she could devote her life to.

Instead, she had chosen to sit for the Indian civil service examinations to join the cadre of public servants that, in those days, controlled everything from the permit for a new factory to the production of bread. The examination turned out to be more a test of endurance than of knowledge and after two years of swotting in candlelit rooms as the state's electricity crisis peaked she took the examination and cleared it.

The next stage was a gruelling interview with a panel of dour-looking men and one woman who she learnt later was a psychologist. Their questions were bewilderingly diverse.

'So, Ms Sen, where do you think Russia is headed? Should they have stopped at Perestroika?' asked a bearded gentlemen.

'What are your views on the Indian cooperative movement?' asked another.

Sohini had been prepared. Information and opinion gleaned from copies of *Time* magazine devoured at the American Center Library, swot books on current affairs and disciplined reading of three newspapers ensured that she cleared the interview.

The Indian civil service follows a strict, inflexible hierarchy where examination and interview rank solely determines whether one makes it to the much-coveted administrative or foreign service or has to settle for a life lower in the pecking order. The candidate has no choice. She fails to make it to the highest tier but the second berth is hers. Thus, Sohini Sen, who as a child had shrieked with fear at the sight of a toy gun and clamped her hands over her ears when her friends shot at balloons with an air rifle, found herself a member of the country's elite police service.

Getting on the list of recruits does not mean that she is handed a gun and a badge. There are five months of training to go through at the academy. She finds herself burning the midnight oil again in her hostel room in a bleak and rocky central Indian city, reading the law, history and police procedure. She hates the arms training, her shots hit feet or even yards away from the target. But the trainers are indulgent towards young women and she gets an 'average' score despite her ineptitude with the gun.

On a June morning that has a hint of rain, she finds herself on a podium on the parade ground saluting a senior officer, the badge of a police officer finally pinned on her starched khaki uniform. Her mother is there for the graduation. She is an academic and has taught English literature at one of her city's women's colleges for decades. In the photographs that Sohini's friends have taken of the ceremony she looks ill at ease, still baffled by her daughter's strange choice of career and overwhelmed by the pomp and pageantry that surround her on this graduation day.

Sohini joins her state cadre and her first tenure is in a town in a placid district in the west of the state. But it was not so placid after all if she cares to remember. The head of a panchayat is brutally murdered and rumours spread that this was a caste killing, somewhat rare in this state but rife in the adjoining state that shares a border with the district. There are auguries of a brewing caste war – crude weapons are being amassed in safe houses and hectoring local politicians are exhorting the slowly swelling audiences at village rallies to take revenge. She apprehends the killer within forty-eight hours. He turns out to be the victim's brother-in-law; the murder is about a land dispute and the caste warriors disband.

She is rewarded for this and she finds herself posted to the coveted crime branch of the state police housed in an Edwardian red brick building in the capital's office district. She discovers that there is a hushed reverence for academic excellence in the service and this gets her some challenging assignments. She handles with quiet efficiency the curious case of a large cache of arms dropped in the middle of a sprawling maze of paddy fields in a district in the state's north-west from an unregistered Russian cargo plane. She arrests the chain-smoking Georgian pilot with his impossibly blue eyes and alcoholic tremor in his hands as well as the ideologue of the fringe left-wing group that these arms were meant for.

In the arcane system of rewards and punishments in the state's police force, an assignment to provide security to its politicians, 'VIP security' as it is termed, is coveted.

She is tentative about accepting this, wary of politicians of every hue, but is advised that spending a few years getting to know people who push and pull the levers of the state machinery would help her in the future. She finds herself in the security detail of Atin Bhadra, the state's home minister who a number of secessionist groups in the north of the state have vowed to kill. At first, Bhadra confirms her worst fears about politicians. He is a short-tempered, foul-mouthed bear of a man, a self-obsessed workaholic.

However, as she tours the flood-ravaged delta with him six months into her posting, she gets to see another side of both Bhadra and politics. They wade to marooned villages, waist-deep in water, and as he hugs an old woman who has lost her family and her meagre chattels in a primeval gesture of empathy, she cannot help but see the tenderness and the pain in his eyes. As the months pass, she can feel a frisson between them that grows into a bond that she can define neither as romantic nor as erotic. He likes to spend time with her, sharing his modest lunch and talking about himself, his understanding of politics and his childhood. He is also eager to listen and when he is there she finds herself babbling like a brook.

She remembers the mid-June evening when the news comes. She is laid up in bed at home with a vicious viral fever as an early monsoon storm ravages the entire state. His helicopter has crashed in the hills of a northern district and the bodies are yet to be recovered. She does not cry, she is too weak to rail against the unfairness of it all but she knows that a brief but important period of her life has come to an end. She had known him for three years.

She spends a couple of years in the governor's mansion that entails her wearing a crisp uniform and going through, zombie-like, a bewildering parade of ceremonies. She pleads with the commissioner to let her return to the crime branch.

As the fog of depression settles on her mind every waking day, she tries to blow it away by reminiscing about her successes in the five years that followed. She remembers the murders at the Dubash steel plant in Singlapur, the arrest of the one-eyed master IED maker with an artist's delicate hands and equally delicate pride, the triple murders in one of the city's most affluent apartment blocks and many more. She is tipped to head the department soon and become the youngest deputy commissioner ever to lead the city's daily battle against crime. Then things change.

---

The attempt to cover up the murder is shockingly clumsy. The marks on the neck of the hanging girl, Swati Mukherjee, clearly point to ligature strangulation using a wire. Even to the untrained eye, these are distinct from the imprint on her neck left by her dupatta that has been used to suspend her corpse from the ceiling. There are livid bruises on her feet suggesting that her body has been dragged. An insomniac neighbour has seen a group of men entering the house at around three in the morning. An enterprising guard has noted down the number of the car that they came in. Although the number plates have been changed in a hurry, it is easily traced.

This is what in local police parlance is known as an 'open and shut' case. There is no Bengali equivalent of this phrase. The evidence trail leads her to Vivek Sethia, a cocky twenty-three-year-old who has since he was seventeen been hauled up by the police on multiple charges of assault, molestation and even arson. (She, however, fails to fathom why the charges had been quickly dropped.) He had regularly been seen in Swati's flat and her neighbours tell her in hushed tones of the vicious rows that they had overheard. The post-mortem report confirms that Swati was three months' pregnant.

Open and shut. She arrests Vivek at nine in the evening from his flat in one of the city's upscale neighbourhoods. She has good news for the city's middle class deeply perturbed by the killing of one of their own. She asks her department's public relations officer to announce that they are well on their way to solving the case.

Then a sequence of events unfolds in a bewildering rush that leads her to finally fathom why Vivek, despite his trail of crime, has never spent even a night in a police lock-up, let alone a prison cell. Her transfer orders come within a day and she is moved from the crime branch to the police training college as a senior faculty member. The case is handed over to a junior officer, Salil Bose. The witnesses miraculously disappear.

Vivek comes from a family that started out as commodity brokers working out of a small katra in the city's oldest wholesale market. They are now one of the largest real estate developers reclaiming the marshes on the eastern fringe of the city to build large apartment blocks. The Sethias are also a major contributor to the ruling party's election coffers and the money comes in hard cash. At election time it is dispatched in security vans to the districts to pay for marquees for rallies, for trucks and buses to transport rally-goers from far-flung villages lured by the promise of a free lunch and occasionally alcohol. The balance of commerce and business is ensured by a strict quid pro quo and no upstart police officer can disturb this equilibrium.

But that is not the end of her banishment to the far peripheries of the police force. Within six months, she is put in charge of civil defence, an auxiliary police comprising a bunch of policemen's helpers, half-cops with a policeman's half-authority.

'I have become excommunicate and anathema, cast away into eternal damnation,' she tells Sajal, jokingly quoting a line from a film that they had seen together at least six times. This, however, describes her situation succinctly – her career as a police detective is decisively over, her professional soul has been cast away.

---

It is her fifth year in the department located on the sixth floor of a crumbling government office block, the walls of the entrance splattered with betel juice and half the windowpanes missing. She has now had enough. She will end all this in Goa.

# 3

# Arjun Sinha

Arjun sits at the prow of a long, narrow boat in the middle of a small river that snakes through the southern half of the district. The river is called Monda. Generally curious by nature, he has nevertheless not bothered to find out the origins of its name. The tediousness of the last three days, the unrelenting heat and the sullen humidity have brought on a stupor. He, a city animal forever complaining of the growing sprawl of concrete, had not expected this. The untrammelled urge of nature to fill every inch of land with wild, lush verdure has induced in him a sense of unease, adding to his enervation. The cycle of growth and decay is quick in these parts and the constant stench of putrefaction has brought on a mild but unshakeable nausea. He has realized that like all city-dwellers he likes nature in small doses – trimmed, pruned and tamed.

There are two other men on the boat. The boatman, Rashid, the enormity of the effort of getting the boat across the river visible in an unchanged rictus on his face as he stands at the rear and pushes back the water with a large oar. This one-oar sculling is tricky and the rhythmic movement around a pivot requires a deftness that only years of accumulated muscle memory can foster. The other occupant of the boat, who is gingerly balanced on one of the three slats that transverse it, is Madan.

Madan is a policeman, as his sweaty, discoloured, once-khaki uniform attests. He has his fair share of notoriety in the local villages not just as a singularly sadistic wife-beater and alcoholic but also as a corrupt bully and henchman of the local legislator. While his occupation and rank entitle him to a firearm, he prefers a long bamboo cane, a lathi that is well polished with notches spread uniformly along its expanse. He has placed this on his paunch.

'How much longer is it?' Madan asks Rashid. Arjun can follow the local dialect although its cadence is different from the city, a low whine running through every sentence making every verbal exchange seem like a row.

'Not long. Another ten minutes or so,' the boatman replies.

'Hurry up,' Madan tells him. 'There's a storm coming.'

Arjun Sinha, inspector in the crime branch of the city's police force, is here to investigate a murder. The entire village, Madan included, believes it was a crime of passion.

The ferocity of the cuts that the murder weapon, possibly a sickle, has inflicted on the victim's throat suggests the kind of blinding hatred that one can bear only against someone one passionately loves. There is more economy of effort in a murder of purpose. The murdered woman, Haseena Mondal, was twenty-six and allegedly in a relationship with Montu Haldar, a twenty-seven-year-old teacher at the secondary school in the village. The paramour has fled and the police station in Bolpur, a few hundred kilometres from here, where his sister lives with her husband and two daughters, has been alerted.

In this part of the world, investigations of a crime of this kind are entirely about talking to neighbours, identifying potential witnesses, sifting through the piles of gossip and rumour that sit heavily around. And finally, if the police are lucky, extracting a confession. Physical torture is common and there is an entire corps of specialists in the state's police force who pride themselves on their ability to inflict pain – the finger breakers, the nail pullers and the skin flayers – all waiting for the opportunity to display their arts. But Arjun is squeamish about these things.

There have been no confessions, and alibis are tight. Montu is not in Bolpur; he is on the run, thwarting every effort of the police forces of the different districts to apprehend him. Arjun dreads the red blot on his year-end confidential assessment that this unsolved case will mark. He decides to try his luck one last time, here on this boat, on this waddling river full to the brim with the monsoon rain.

---

Haseena happens to be the boatman Rashid's wife. Ever since Arjun's arrival, Rashid has been silent – a cuckold's sullenness tinged with the grief of a recent widower. At the approximate time of death (this is Madan's assessment), Rashid claims to have been in the big city with his nephew Jia (short for the more weighty Zia Ul) to see his unani doctor for the gout-like condition that has inflicted his right knee.

Arjun's intuition, honed by years of meticulous police work, has told him that something is amiss in this neat story of the fugitive paramour and the absent husband. Madan suspects that the killer had an accomplice who had held the victim down when she was so brutally attacked. He had seen prominent bruise marks on her lower legs and knees that would have been difficult for a single assailant to inflict while hacking away at her throat.

Arjun knows he can use it to force a closure of this case even if it flouts the rule book. In these backwaters no one cares, or can afford to care, for rules. The boat has almost reached the bank and he unzips his small travel bag and fishes out an improvised underpant, a langot, a strip of cloth with strings at the extremities that, if tied with dexterity, can function as a sturdy loincloth. He has picked it up from the underbrush behind Rashid's house. Once white, it has acquired a brownish hue due to frequent washes in the muddy river. On it are distinct rust-coloured blotches that on closer inspection reveal themselves to be bloodstains. Arjun holds it aloft and in a voice quivering with the effort of handling the sudden rush from his adrenals, says to Rashid, 'It's all over, Rashid. Jia has confessed. We know this is your langot and so will the judge who sends you to the gallows.'

Rashid's face dissolves into anguish. Then his body is racked with sobs, which build up into an animal howl. 'Hujoor,' he somehow manages to say, 'save me. *Aami khoon korechi.*' (I have murdered.) Madan, dazed for about half a minute, scrambles to his feet to arrest Rashid.

---

As he alights from the boat, Arjun's cellphone, starved of a network connection for the past three days, comes alive. They must be close to a cellphone tower. It immediately starts ringing in an unfussy monotone and he recognizes his office phone number.

The voice at the other end gives a terse command. 'I don't know where you are but get on the first local train that you can catch. Run to the station if you have to. The commissioner wants to see you as soon as possible. It has something to do with the chief minister's office.'

# 4

# The Summons

Sohini's landline phone rings, a low electronic beep that rouses her from her reverie. She assumes it is Brinda, her garrulous niece who works at the front desk of a city hotel. Brinda with her scatterbrained plans of taking Sohini and her mother out on weekends to some of the priciest new restaurants in the city. The dimly lit older restaurants with their worn upholstery and butter-laden Anglo-Indian food won't do for her. Sohini has been raised by her mother on a staple of sermons on the virtues of parsimony and hates the idea of Brinda spending large fractions of her meagre salary on this unnecessary indulgence. She is determined to dissuade her.

'What is it now, Brinda?' she asks.

But it is not Brinda. The man's voice at the other end of the line is not familiar but she recognizes the tone. It is that of a lowly government clerk, muted by years of obsequiousness, of following orders rather than giving them.

'Madam,' he says, 'CM saheb wants to see you immediately. He has given time at six.'

The message is so unexpected that it takes a while to seep through the lingering fog of alcohol. She takes some time to fully comprehend this.

'Madam,' the voice takes on an entreating whine.

'I'll be there,' Sohini replies.

It is five minutes past four and by the time she washes down two aspirins with a cup of foul chicory-rich coffee, gets back into her khaki uniform and summons her driver, Ram Bahadur, a Nepali from Darjeeling, half an hour has passed. The journey from the southern neighbourhood that has been her home for the past three decades to the state government's headquarters housed in a sprawling colonial building in the heart of the city takes long. A protest rally on the main avenue that connects the city's southern extremities to its centre has brought traffic to a standstill. A slow drizzle that blurs the windshield and the steady, slightly screechy pulse of the wipers add to her agitation. It is almost six and she is still a couple of kilometres away from her destination. She borrows Ram Bahadur's umbrella and decides to walk.

She reaches the building a good twenty minutes late, her nerves jangling from the relentless blaring of car horns, aching from the contortions she had to put her fatigued, unexercised body through to weave her way in and out of the throng of pedestrians. As she reaches the gate, she sees the reassuring face of Subhendubabu, the minister's personal assistant, waiting at the entrance for her. She tries to apologize for her tardiness but he will have none of it.

'It's not your fault. You had to come at such short notice,' he says. Kind, avuncular Subhendubabu, patron of the ingénues in the state's male-dominated bureaucracy, was one of the few people who had telephoned her after her fall from grace and apologized for his inability to help. She hopes he will assuage her curiosity a little by telling her what this urgent summons is all about. But he remains silent and Sohini knows that it is wise not to ask questions.

As they walk down the corridor, she is assailed by the smell of overbrewed tea that comes from the small tea shops that flank her path. This part of the building has the atmosphere of a fair in full swing. There is a lottery-seller hawking the Sikkim government's lottery, a man selling entrance forms for competitive exams from a makeshift table and a woman hawking boiled homemade lozenges. The white walls have bright red stains of freshly spat betel juice and are haphazardly splattered with posters, mostly of the myriad trade unions that the building's army of clerks patronize.

—

As they get closer to the chief minister's office, the corridors are cleaner and free of peddlers. It is dark outside now and across the road she can see the small lake shimmering with the reflection of the yellow street lights and the neon signs. Finally, through a small room meant for waiting guests, she is ushered into the chief minister's office. He sits across a long horseshoe table covered in a green fabric that she associates with billiard tables which in turn is covered in glass. In this sanctum sanctorum of the state's power, the minister looks diminutive in his crumpled Panjabi and, through the thick glasses he wears, she can make out the exhaustion in his eyes, red-rimmed and puffy, possibly from reading the stacks of files that he has cleared through the day. Or has he been crying?

He asks her to sit and wastes no time on pleasantries.

'You must have heard of Ronen Chatterjee, the chairman of Dubash Industries,' the minister says.

'Yes, I have,' she replies. Dubash and Company are one of the biggest conglomerates in the state with interests in construction, steel and cement. One of the few Parsi investors in the state in the first decade of the twentieth century, the Dubashes had seen their fortunes soar in the jute boom of the First World War and they had ploughed their pickings first into steel and then cement. Their record of philanthropy and excellent labour relations had insulated them from the political turbulence of the late sixties that had rocked the state. Now a publicly owned company with shares listed in both Mumbai and New York, their headquarters, an architectural icon of the city, is visible from the chief minister's office.

'Ronen's daughter, Ahona,' the minister pauses for a moment, 'she was killed last night in her flat. It was particularly brutal from what I hear.'

He continues but his voice trembles with the effort of harnessing his emotions.

'Ronen and I were classmates in school. I know,' tears well up as he corrects himself, 'I knew her since she was born. I want you to investigate the case. I want results quickly. I have spoken to the police commissioner and he has arranged for a temporary office at the crime branch. You will of course have the support of the entire department but there is an officer who will work with you only on this case. I think he is waiting outside for you.'

A nod from the minister and the light touch of Subhendubabu on her arm and she realizes that her audience is over. As the disorientation this urgent and wholly unexpected summons has induced slowly fades and the fatigue of negotiating the early evening traffic and the commuters on the pavements lifts, the realization that her career has been resurrected sinks in.

Sohini leaves the office with the obvious question of why a clapped-out, fading police officer like her is being asked to head what could turn out to be a high-profile investigation dogging her. She thinks of asking Subhendubabu, who is escorting her out, but desists.

Outside in the corridor, a man in his early forties wearing a white bush shirt and black trousers is waiting for her. She recognizes him as one of the detectives who had helped her in the arms-drop case. She remembers him as the victim of a deep personal tragedy. Oh yes, his young wife, son and father had been run over by a speeding truck right outside their home. She remembers his earnestness and eagerness to please her during the probe.

Her reinduction into the great machine of power insidiously brings on an imperiousness that is associated with hierarchy and rank. She dispenses with the various parts of speech that combine to form a full sentence. Instead, she asks in Bengali, 'Name?'

'Arjun Sinha,' comes the reply.

# 5

# The Crime Scene

Police manuals across the world stipulate that the first step of a murder investigation should be a visit to the crime scene. One can speculate on whether there is indeed a better way to start a probe. But this is the norm and this city is no exception. Thus at seven-thirty in the evening, Arjun and Sohini find themselves under the makeshift canvas shelter of a tea stall outside the state headquarters. The drizzle has now become a steady downpour. They are headed for Ahona Chatterjee's flat. Arjun steps out intermittently from under the canopy to wave wildly at passing black-and-yellow cabs. However, finding one seems particularly difficult that evening.

Ram Bahadur has not reached the state secretariat with Sohini's police car and Arjun's modest white Alto is parked at the crime branch headquarters about a kilometre away.

The swell of people bound homeward from the protest march has spilled over into the streets and has resulted in a gridlock. At last, an empty cab stops, and asks for a premium over the meter fare which they reluctantly agree to pay. By eight they are on their way to the crime scene in a southern neighbourhood. The taxi driver has driven on these streets long enough to know the warren of lanes and by-lanes that skirt the city's arterial avenues and so they miraculously manage to evade the snarl of traffic that has held up Ram Bahadur.

—

Ahona Chatterjee's neighbourhood fetches among the highest prices in the city per square foot of space and is really a single lane ending in a cul de sac. It is flanked on both sides by sprawling mansions usually with a lawn and a garden. Some are colonial while the others have a more modern architecture. It has not entirely escaped the attention of real estate sharks. The attempt to convert two of the old buildings into a large residential complex has been thwarted by a court injunction in response to a public interest litigation from an NGO intent on preserving the city's architectural heritage.

Her flat is in a relatively new building that has a curious layout. The ground floor comprises two flats, one large three-bedroom flat with another long, narrow one running by its side with a single bedroom, a kitchen and a living room. The bathroom is right next to the entrance. It is the quintessence of a bachelor pad and is, or was, Ahona's home. Her body has been found in her living room.

The main door to this small flat is on the side and can be reached by a concrete path flanked by slivers of grass and a couple of flower beds. Unlike most of the other buildings, which are fronted by their lawns, this has its sprawl of green at the back. A small trellised iron gate opens into the concrete path. The adjacent flat is between tenants, the previous occupants having moved to Dubai and the new incumbents yet to arrive. A caretaker comes in during the day but locks up by five. The first floor is occupied by the bedridden eighty-three-year-old Mrs Talukdar, and her nurse who is past sixty. She is the mother of the late U.C. Talukdar, once a flamboyant shipping tycoon but long dead, his alleged suicide while serving time in a Mumbai jail for maritime insurance fraud the subject of many a canard. The old lady has refused to sell her flat despite increasingly dire financial conditions.

Some of the houses have guards. They have quaint kiosks at their entrance, all painted the same shade of green in a surprising show of conformity. Perhaps it is the only shade of the kind of waterproof paint that is available. The kiosks, however, offer scant protection against anything more than a drizzle and when it rains harder the guards find sanctuary either in the garages in the main building or in the row of quarters meant for the household help.

As their cab turns into the mouth of the alley, Sohini and Arjun notice a row of police cars including two refurbished Black Marias parked next to the curb. As they reach Ahona's building, they also see at least three OB vans of the city's major television channels. The entrance to the flat is well lit by spotlights that both the police and the television crews have brought along. There are police spotlights inside the flat to scour it for evidence.

Things are busy outside. Television reporters clad in old-fashioned plastic raincoats are barking into their microphones while some ambitious cameramen are bargaining with the police sentries to wangle a camera shot of the flat's interior. Then there is the usual gaggle of onlookers, some with umbrellas and others braving the rain. Like extras in a film's crowd scene, they offer themselves as voluntary props that always complete a crime or accident scene. Drawn mostly from the city's underclass, they are textbook voyeurs – quiet, unobtrusive but always watching. Any spectacle – a murder, a grisly accident or simply a large crane demolishing an old building with a wrecking ball – attracts them like flies to syrup. Sohini uses a Bengali word for them – dorshok or spectators – and has always wondered where they come from and what secret homing device they use to always arrive at the right spot.

Police textbooks might insist that a murder probe begins with the crime scene but in this part of the world only the most inexperienced of investigators would hope to get ready clues. Contamination, to use the jargon of forensic scientists, tends to be high and often the visit is a mere formality.

This murder is no different. The local policemen, the first to arrive on the scene after the body's discovery at ten in the morning, have trampled all over the living room where the body was found, leaving behind their own footprints and fingerprints, obliterating the possibility of finding these human traces of the killer. The body was first seen by Ahona's maid, Maya. Her hysterical screams had attracted the neighbourhood guards, who have added to the desecration. Their muddy bootprints are all over the flat and follow a curious, random pattern suggesting a nervous scampering about by their owners, shocked and frightened no doubt at the sight of the corpse.

The decapitation has not been complete and when discovered the head was hanging forward – as if in deep prayer or in a gesturc of penitence – held by the uncut neck muscles. One of the young constables, brave enough to attempt to move the bloodless head back into its correct anatomical position, was overcome by a wave of nausea and has vomited right next to the corpse. After hastily covering the body with a white sheet, a sweeper has been called to sweep the area, and precious evidence along with it.

Sohini believes that she has never been to a house that gives as little away about its owner as Ahona's flat. The furniture is expensive but seems to have been picked out absent-mindedly from a catalogue. The paintings and posters seem like an afterthought and are so varied that they reveal nothing about the owner's taste. The bookshelf has an equally varied collection. There is Ovid and Homer, possibly textbooks from Ahona's undergraduate course, a Nadine Gordimer and an Updike along with cheap thrillers, two dictionaries and a variety of cookbooks.

The bedroom is tidy. The bedspread has a familiar Indian motif and, on opening the chest of drawers, Sohini finds five or six almost identical ones. Her clothes seem to suggest something of a personal style – they are all long-sleeved dark kurtas.

What really surprises Sohini after a thorough search of the flat is the absence of any medicines. The ubiquitous box that all households seem to have containing a half-empty bottle of Dettol and pills to bring down a sudden fever in the middle of the night or soothe a dyspeptic stomach is missing. She looks carefully again and finds nothing. She instructs the crime scene constables to look harder.

She then talks to the forensic expert, Durgababu, about the forensic team's work. They had arrived at around noon after the local station informed the branch and have been at work since. Durga Charan Maity (DCM to his colleagues) is a crime branch veteran. He retired almost a decade ago but has been kept on as a consultant for his skills and his unmatched experience of investigating at least three hundred murders. In the world of forensic science, where new specializations sprout like mushrooms, Maity would have the lowly rank of crime scene investigator. His colleagues, however, know that he is much more than that. Although he lacks formal training in forensics except for a few workshops that he has attended, over the years he has mastered the diversities of this dismal science. He knows enough about anatomy, pathology and toxicology to be able to fill in for an absent doctor. He has a deep understanding of ballistics and the tricky geometry it involves, and his vast experience has left him with a clinical insight into the human mind. He is one of the few generalists left in a world where others like to stay blockaded in their small fiefs of narrow expertise like insecure satraps. For the crime branch, he is the go-to guy, their search engine. A cocky young inspector, evidently a Hitchcock fan, had once described his role succinctly: 'Dial DCM for murder.'

DCM has never married and possesses the attributes that Bengalis like in their bachelors. He is tall, at least six inches above the ethnic average, and is fastidious about his clothes. He keeps his flat clean, cooks himself, and years of regular exercise have kept a potbelly, the bane of the ageing Bengali male, at bay. This, despite the fact that his evening diet comprises three large pegs of Old Monk rum mixed with tepid water. That he was a boxer in his youth and has represented his state in the sport adds to his mystique.

Like many of his generation, DCM carries the taint of police atrocities in the late sixties and early seventies when the state waged war on its young. As a rookie in the crime branch, he vividly remembers the bodies heaped together like sacks of potato in the back of a truck, bullet marks on their backs and occasionally the piercing made by a large hook used to haul gunny bags, an innovative tool of torture of the time. He is reluctant to discuss this and, when the topic surfaces, all he says is, 'We couldn't afford to care for the human rights of those who didn't care for it themselves. Did you know that those bastards killed innocent traffic constables?'

Unlike his colleagues who either fattened on promotions or succumbing to the indolence of middle age spent their fifties as bureaucratic drones and severed their connections with policing after retiring, Durga Maity has kept pace with the rapid change in the technology of forensics. Often the lack of resources has meant that its tools have been beyond his reach. But this hasn't quite bothered him. DCM knows the limits of technology and the pitfalls of dependence on its cycle of constant obsolescence and innovation. His own instruments have always been an acute sense of observation, a strong intuition and an ability to use a logical train of thought to fit together disparate pieces of evidence.

---

Sohini is engrossed in her conversation with DCM, carefully listening to every detail of his briefing on the forensic team's work. Then, without warning, in the span of a few seconds, the enclosed flat, bloodstains on the floor, the distinct metallic and sweet smell of blood and the overworked spotlights adding to the trapped, muggy atmosphere seem to close in on her. It is not mere physical revulsion at the gore in the room and the corpse's photograph that Durgababu is displaying on the police photographer's digital camera. She has seen worse. This is more an acute fear of being ensnared again in a life that she has left far behind, a life she lacks the confidence, or the will, to go through again. She abruptly ends the conversation and walks out into the rain. After a couple of minutes she breaks into a trot with her hands rolled into tight fists in her pocket and heads for the main avenue from where she hopes to find a taxi home. She needs a drink and her pills desperately.

'Is madam all right?' Durgababu asks Arjun, who is visibly surprised by Sohini's unannounced exit.

'I think so...she probably needs to call bodosaheb,' he improvises, referring to the police commissioner.

'There is no sign of forced entry so we can presume that Ahona knew the killer,' Durgababu tells Arjun. 'This was an intelligent killer with a fair idea of how forensics work. Of course, the fuckers from the local station and the guards have buggered up the flat so badly that even if we called in all of Scotland Yard they wouldn't be able to find anything useful. I couldn't lift any fingerprints or footprints from the bathroom either but I suspect he might have washed off the blood from the carotid that would have sprayed him. I saw traces of bloody finger- and footmarks but both his feet and hands seem to have been sheathed in some kind of glove or sock so that there are no real prints. I remember seeing a Michael Douglas [he pronounces it Doglas] film years ago. I don't remember the story now, but it was called *The Perfect Murder*. We might just have a perfect murder on our hands.'

The reference to the UK's elite crime force carries a sense of irony, of wounded pride. The city's crime branch was known as the Scotland Yard of the East but years of poor funding and political interference have wiped off that sheen.

'Did the doctor say anything about the time of death?' asks Arjun.

'You know how these fellows work. Always covering their arses! I forced him and only then did he give me an approximate time. It could have been any time between nine and midnight. The poor fellow was so spooked by the sight of the corpse that he could barely bring himself to touch the body. I wonder from where we get these amateurs.'

'Has anyone spoken to the neighbours or the guards? Did they notice anything?' Arjun asks.

'Do you seriously expect anyone to come forward even if he had sat down for a cup of tea with the killer?' Durgababu replies. 'The bahadurs claim to have been inside their compounds because of the rain. The people who live in these mansions are too hoity-toity to even bother to talk to us. If you ring their doorbell, they threaten to call the commissioner and complain of police harassment. The guards are, however, all certain that they did not hear a car arrive nor see any leave after nine. They did say that she had two regular male visitors. Her brother turned up often and a bearded bloke who visited frequently for about three months.'

Durgababu's cynicism about finding witnesses is legitimate. When it comes to helping the police with a murder investigation or an accident this country becomes the land of the blind. There could be a murder in broad daylight in the heart of a busy market and yet no witnesses are likely to come forward. Attempts at coercing them are invariably met with a sullen, resolute silence that even the most intimidating or patient policeman finds impossible to penetrate. This is for a reason. There is virtually no credible witness protection scheme in the country, no comfortable safe house with a warm bed and microwave where a witness can be holed up until the criminal is safely put away. The fear of retribution runs high.

The lack of safe haven is one side of the story. Arjun knows very well that there is a deep fear of police and judicial harassment. Offer to help the forces of law in any way and you could find yourself drawn into the byzantine corridors of their bureaucracy. The umpteenth summons to the court could mean a loss of another day's wages; yet another visit to the police station and the pressure to tweak an eyewitness account to one that is more convenient to the police, the loss of a night's sleep.

Arjun picks up the digital camera again and scrolls through the photographs. 'What are these marks on her arms and thighs?' he asks Durgababu.

'Self-mutilation,' he replies. 'I have seen these in suicide cases. Apparently comes from an unbearable loathing of oneself. The human mind is so difficult to fathom. Can you imagine someone sitting quietly somewhere and doing this to herself...' His voice trails off.

Arjun realizes that the long, dark kurtas are not Ahona's signature style. She wore them to mask these marks of self-harm.

He finally steps out of the flat at a quarter past ten and into a police car that offers him a ride home. He calls Sohini on her mobile phone. He expects some apology or simply an acknowledgement of the awkwardness of her sudden exit. He gets neither.

'Let's meet the parents tomorrow morning at their flat at ten,' she tells him matter-of-factly.

The pills and three pegs of vodka have done their work. Sohini is in charge again.

# 6

# The Parents

In his fifteen years of working for the crime branch, Arjun has become inured to the idea of murder. The motives and methods that blur the line between the human and bestial have long ceased to fascinate him. They have become predictable, conforming to a template that some probing and a bit of luck always reveal. Yet he remains obsessed with the myriad expressions of grief that come in the wake of an unnatural death. He feels that these expressions, if analysed carefully, offer useful clues, although some of his colleagues warn him that this might mar his judgement.

For Sohini, this interview is a giant leap from her periodic inspection of the home guards with their overwashed khaki uniforms and eager salutes. She is edgy and keen to get on. They reach the Chatterjees' house in an affluent south-western neighbourhood. It is a six-storeyed building, built in the sixties, with a large driveway and a large lawn at the back. In today's space-starved architectural plans, each storey would have at least four flats. But this was built in a time of abundance. Only a few like the Chatterjees can afford to hold on to these relics of an older, less populous city.

Ahona's father, Ronen, meets them at the lift that stops at a small passage that separates the private areas of the house – three bedrooms and a small study – from the dining and living rooms. The living room decor is soothingly tasteful, soothing for Sohini since it does not have a trace of ostentation. The walls are lined with bookshelves bearing well-worn books that have clearly been read. These are quite unlike the pristine leather-bound and gilt-spined tomes that she has seen in other affluent homes, their purpose solely to decorate. There is an old but well-preserved Bang & Olufsen player next to the record shelf that has a large number of neatly stacked records. A number of paintings, mostly abstract modern work, adorn the wall.

Sajal's company has taught Sohini the rudiments of Indian art. She recognizes some paintings of the Bombay school on the Chatterjees' walls that would fetch quite a sum at today's prices. She finds her gaze turning to a poster of an exhibition held a few years ago at a London gallery, of the Dutch portraitist Hans Holbein, that occupies the sliver of a wall between the bookshelves and the windows. It is a portrait of a dour man wearing a black cap.

'It's Thomas More. Holbein spent a lot of time at Henry

VIII's court,' says Ronen, referring to the subject of the painting as he follows the line of her gaze. 'Boori, I mean Ahona, went for that exhibition with us.'

Sohini guesses that Boori was Ahona's pet name. It means old woman; its literal inappropriateness as a description of a child notwithstanding, it is popular among Bengalis, an example of the race's quirky sense of humour. The only thing that Sohini remembers from her high school history textbook is that Thomas More was decapitated. She wonders if there is irony in this and whether Ronen is aware of it.

Arjun has heard of neither Henry VIII nor Thomas More but is both surprised and somewhat impressed by Ronen's ability to make polite conversation in his emotional state.

Ronen is short even by Bengali standards but, despite being in his mid sixties, retains a spryness and musculature that regular games of tennis and swimming have ensured. He is clad in linen, appropriate for this time of the year. He is almost completely bald. This is a curse of heredity and he has had to tolerate the nickname 'Baldy Chatterjee' that his more anglicized friends at the club had given him since his early forties. There is impatience – or is it arrogance, Sohini wonders – writ on his clean-shaven, round face. She believes it is indeed the arrogance of power, the utter contempt for the prospect of answering questions put to him by people who are perhaps five scales below his pay grade. He would much rather have them scouring the city's streets looking for his daughter's killer than sit in his living room, asking him questions about his private life.

The scion of a family of absentee landlords that had lived in the city since the early nineteenth century off the fat of their large tracts of land in a faraway eastern district, Ronen is one of the few remaining professionals who were educated in England and returned to join a firm in this city. Unlike many of their peers whom dissolute lifestyles and an utter disregard for the future had driven to penury, the Chatterjee family had remained solvent. The returns from their investments, first in railway bonds that the colonial government floated to lay the vast networks of tracks that traverse this country and then in blue-chip company shares, funded Ronen's studies at Cambridge. He has fond memories of his three years in the small university town that he spent largely in the company of other Indian students, cooking together, serendipitously discovering local substitutes for Indian ingredients at the local grocer, occasionally punting on the Cam and listening to debates at the Indian Majlis.

He belongs to the last crop of the more genteel manager class that ran the city's corporations before the coiled aggression that the new American-style business school graduates learnt became the norm. His generation, the boxwallahs, raised on a routine of gin and tonics on Friday afternoons and golf at the weekends, managed some of the last of the old and tottering British agencies until they went into decline. In the mid eighties, after a tea company that Ronen managed threatened to go belly-up, he joined the Dubashes, the last of the city's surviving old industrial mammoths, as a mid-level manager and has been with them ever since.

Nayantara Chatterjee (or Nonnie as her friends call her, this anglicized abbreviation acquired during her schooldays), Ahona's mother, is seated on a sofa upholstered in a self-patterned muted cream fabric. She is taller than her husband, wears her hair straight and like her husband hasn't allowed age to take a toll on her body. In her fight against the ravages of time she has yoga as her ally that she both practises with the unflinching regularity of a monk and teaches to a small group of friends. She is clad in a plain cotton sari. Her face is long, almost equine, toned, with high cheekbones that the light coming in from the window accentuates.

Nonnie comes from a different background. Her family was from the vast Bengali professional diaspora that had sought their fortunes in the North. Her father was a doctor in Lahore who fled the horrors of Partition with his family and set up a practice in Kailash Colony in Delhi, a settlement for refugees from across the border. While her father's new practice gave him a renewed sense of purpose, her mother lapsed into a permanent state of what Nonnie had read Victorian novels describe as 'melancholia'. She later found out this was acute clinical depression that was barely recognized as a disease given the medical science of the day. A few years ago she had learnt from her family physician that it was hereditary, could skip a generation and was beginning to cast a shadow on Ahona's mind.

Ronen Chatterjee is in control of himself, his grief private and contained. Nayantara too seems to be making an effort to harness her emotions but both Sohini and Arjun sense that her grief is tinged with a seething anger, a need to pound her fists, to hurt, to blame rather than give in to the helplessness of sorrow.

Their clothes and their bearing mark a stark contrast to Arjun and Sohini. Sohini is dressed in a man's short-sleeved shirt and black trousers. Her lack of exercise and dependence on alcohol and prescription drugs (consumed far beyond prescribed limits) has aged her beyond her years. Her pageboy haircut looks to be the work of an amateur and has done little to mask the gauntness of her face. Arjun does his daily calisthenics but has a limited wardrobe. He is clad in a light blue shirt that frequent washes have turned almost white with a pair of crushed khaki pants that clearly haven't been ironed in a while.

---

Sohini has always found it difficult to offer condolences. The hollowness of any words that she could offer to assuage or empathize deters her from going through this ritual. She gets straight to the point.

'Why was Ahona living on her own?' she asks the parents.

Ronen replies, 'She was always an independent person. Fiercely independent, I might add. By the time she was eighteen she wanted her own place. She kicked up a real fuss about this. So finally, when she turned twenty, we let her have her way. We have had the small flat for a good twenty years now. We bought it as an investment. Incidentally, we insisted that Boori's maid, Maya, who has been with us since she was a baby, stay with her. But on most evenings Boori would pack her off to her daughter's house that is fairly close to the flat. There was very little either Nonnie or I could do about it.'

The next question from Sohini is straight out of a policing textbook. 'Can you think of anyone who could bear a grudge against you or Nonnie strong enough to commit this crime?'

Ronen's voice trembles as he tries to harness the anger that rises at the sheer absurdity of the question. 'Ms Sen,' he replies, 'I work for a company that makes cement and steel. It's not the mafia. I might have enemies or people who don't like me. I had a big row with my club's secretary a couple of days back, for example. I'm certain that there is no love lost between us. But my enemies, as you prefer to call them, are not the kind who would chop my daughter's head off because of a vendetta against me. As for Ahona, she was twenty-three, for god's sake, and the very idea of someone bearing a grudge so deep seems ridiculous.'

Sohini persists. 'Do you have frequent rows with other

people like the club secretary you mentioned? Have you been physically violent with anyone?'

This question is meant to unnerve Ronen, to provoke him into an outburst that could reveal what lies behind his carefully crafted veneer. He, however, does not rise to the bait and chooses not to answer the question though quite clearly he is enraged. Arjun can see the whites of the knuckles of his right hand as he grips the sofa's armrest. Good cop, bad cop. The policeman's pantomime. Arjun realizes that it is time to play the foil to Sohini.

'How did she find her work? Did she make a lot of friends there?' he asks to leaven the atmosphere.

It is Nayantara's turn to answer. She has a rasp in her voice, the kind associated with many decades of regular smoking. Her Bengali accent still has some inflections of Hindi, the language she spoke as a child with her friends. She, like many of her class and upbringing, is more comfortable in English, which she speaks with grammatical correctness and in complete sentences, a rarity these days.

'Ahona was always a bit of a loner. She didn't make friends easily. The few that she had were from her school. Shefali was possibly closest to her and they were together since nursery and went to the same college. Others like Jeroo, Mr Dubash's daughter, and Minnie left the city after school. But she seemed perfectly happy at work.'

'Was she in a relationship with a man?' Sohini asks.

Nonnie answers this. 'She was always secretive about

these things. But I know of one boy that she seemed quite friendly with – Saikat. This started about six months ago. Unfortunately, they seem to have broken up now. She had always been close to her brother, Shonjoy. In fact, he is here now.'

'Can we speak to him?' Arjun asks.

'He is a little overwrought. As I said, he was very close to his sister and the shock of her death has affected him badly. Besides, he went and identified her body at that ghastly morgue at the medical college. But let me try calling him.'

She gestures to a manservant who has been lurking outside the room for a while, wondering if the occasion is appropriate to ask if the guests wanted tea or coffee, and then continues, 'You might think I am a terrible mother, Ms Sen. Ahona was our only daughter. Yet, here I am, sitting and answering questions without breaking down. I feel guilty about this. But the fact is that this is the way I have been brought up – not to make a show of things that I believe are deeply private. Besides, I am honest about the fact that she and I had drifted apart over the years.'

Ronen, seated next to her, touches her upper arm in a show of both affection and solidarity. 'You don't need to explain yourself like this,' he says gently.

The kettle boils over. The dam bursts. Nonnie's voice rises a few decibels, an angry shrillness cuts through her rasp.

'Ronen, don't tell me what I need or needn't do. It is time someone took the responsibility for what has happened. Our only daughter is dead, Ronen. Has that registered in your brain or do you need a memo from Mr Dubash to make you aware of what we've lost? I was a poor mother to her – I am willing to take the blame for that, repent for the rest of my life. But what about you? Your decisions are responsible for Boori's grisly death. You have treated our children like the workers at your factories. If they are unhappy and threaten to strike, give them a good raise and things will blow over. You don't bring children up like that.'

Ronen is meek in his reply. 'If you think my decision to let Boori live on her own caused her death, then I take full responsibility for it if that pleases you.'

'You know very well that's not the only thing I am blaming you for, Ronen, but let's leave it at that.'

Sohini waits for a few moments for the hostility to end before she continues her questioning. 'We noticed marks on her thighs and arms, possibly cuts made by a blade or small knife. These have nothing to do with the murder but I was wondering if you were aware of this.'

Ronen answers this question very carefully. 'Ahona wasn't just independent and feisty. She was also very disturbed. She used to cut herself with a blade. We forced her to see a psychiatrist. I don't know the exact medical term for it but the doctor said that depressed people harm themselves at times.'

Nayantara interrupts. She has regained some of her composure but there is still a residue of harshness in her voice. 'My mother was clinically depressed for almost half her life. I am sorry to put it like this but she lived the life of a vegetable. Dr Ghosh, our family physician, told me that Ahona's illness could have been passed on from my mother.'

---

At this moment, Shonjoy enters the room. He does not have the self-control of his parents. He has obviously been crying and his hands have a noticeable tremor. What, however, is most striking about him is his expression. Though they see him but briefly, both detectives sense the loss of equilibrium in him, a tipping of the mind's finely calibrated scales.

'I am not feeling too well,' he stammers. 'Can we speak later? I could come down to the station in the evening if you want.'

Sohini is surprisingly kind. Good cop now. 'Call us when you are feeling a little better. I will leave our numbers. We can come down here or to your flat if you like.'

'Yes, I would like Atreyi to be around when we meet.'

Ronen tells them that Atreyi is Shonjoy's wife of four years. They are both bankers but they work in different banks. They have the right pedigree, having graduated from one of the better business schools in the country. For professionals like them, this city is a backwater, a punishment posting. The demise of industry has meant a weak appetite for money. The small affluent class is averse to risk and remains unmoved by the promises of enrichment that bankers offer. There is an emerging parvenu class that is more accepting of the vagaries of the financial world but every banker wants to woo them. Competition is thus fierce. Atreyi wants to leave this city and move to one of the many metropolises where the clichéd economic boom of this country is more visible.

Sohini asks them what they were doing on the night of the murder. 'This is just routine,' she explains.

Ronen and Nonnie were at their club with friends and had returned late. They have an alibi: a couple that lives in the same neighbourhood had asked them for a lift. Shonjoy, however, does not have one. After work that ended at six, he had played a few games of badminton at the racquet club until seven-thirty after which he had shared a bottle of beer with his friend Atul. He left the club at eight and claims to have driven by the river for an hour or so before taking a long route back to his empty flat and having dinner in front of the television. Atreyi was away in Mumbai on work. He says he drives by the river often without purpose or destination to clear his head and straighten his thoughts.

Before they leave they take Saikat's and Shefali's phone numbers. Nonnie has one of Ahona's business cards with her office address and the board number. She worked for a small but well-known publishing house with its office in one of the new blocks that have come up on the city's eastern fringes. Nonnie scribbles down the name of Ahona's supervisor at the back.

On their way out, Ronen takes Sohini into the study. He speaks softly but with intensity. 'Ms Sen, you might be wondering why you have been suddenly brought back from your long exile. Let me tell you. I have followed your career closely through Ahin Mitra, your father's friend who happens to be my lawyer. I followed the Sethia case – how you were punished instead of being rewarded for doing your job well. I specifically wanted you on this case. I spoke to the chief minister myself and I got Mr Dubash to speak to the home secretary in Delhi to get you reinstated in the crime branch. As you understand all too well, Ms Sen, every crime is being politicized these days. God knows what spin the press and the police might put on this. My company will be dragged into it and, for all you know, my wife and I could be put behind bars. Don't smile, Ms Sen, this is no exaggeration. It has happened to others, people of our class and background. I am banking on the fact that you will not succumb to any pressure.'

Sohini is surprisingly quick in her reply. 'So you do have enemies, Ronenbabu! Besides, what makes you think I will not cave in to pressure?'

Ronen is equally quick to answer. 'I think you are one of the few police officers remaining in the force who are interested in the truth. I am sure you recall the Singlapur murders where two of our workers were murdered inside the factory gates. Both Mr Dubash and I remember how you stood up to Arun Barman, the local MP who tried to frame us for not letting his union into our company. You put his son-in-law behind bars.

'Let me put it this way,' he continues. 'If we think you are playing some kind of game with us, Mr Dubash and I will make sure that you return to the hellhole of a department that you have been stuck in for the last five years. You have nothing to gain from doing someone's bidding. On the flip side, you have nothing to lose by finding out the truth about my daughter's murder.'

---

Sohini and Arjun drive by the river on their way to their makeshift office at the crime branch. This is the same road that Shonjoy claims to have taken on the night of his sister's murder. They are in Sohini's white Ambassador. Ram Bahadur is still grumpy from his encounter with the traffic the previous evening. After sitting in a virtually static car for over two hours, his bladder had protested and he had to face the ignominy of pissing into a bush that flanked the closest pavement in full view of what he thinks were millions of commuters.

It has stopped raining. The sun is out and a haze rises from the river. The buildings on the other side of the river, the city's industrial suburb, seem like a mirage threatening to disappear if one got any closer. The outline of the cantilever bridge, a mesh of grey steel, an enduring icon of the city, becomes slowly visible through the haze. Arjun remembers taking his son for the cheap ferry rides across the river used mostly by commuters to the city from its suburbs. Unlike the commuters, they did not get off the ferry and kept chugging back and forth. Every time Arjun tried to get off the boat at the pier on the city side his son would throw a tantrum, his shrill voice screaming, *'Abar, abar!'* (Again, again!)

They reach the crime branch headquarters. The ceiling fan in their shared office has been acting up, stopping suddenly with a loud groan and then starting as suddenly with a piercing shriek and rotating at a frightening speed. Arjun leaves to look for their famously elusive office electrician.

Sohini wants to know more about the Chatterjees and she thinks of Ahin Mitra. He is the friend that Ronen mentioned who also knew her long-dead father. She knows that Ahinkaku, as she calls him, has kept in touch with her mother and that he has always made it a point to ask about her. He is a successful lawyer and in this city where litigation is a passion is usually busy and impossible to reach during the day. She calls her mother for his number. Mercifully the courts are in recess and he picks up after the first ring.

He is reticent, reluctant to discuss his close friends' private lives at this time of distress. When she insists that it would help her get closer to the truth about Ahona's death, he relents but is guarded in his response. He tends to meander, philosophize and lapse into generalities.

'You've never married, Sohini,' he says. 'But I'm sure that

you are aware of the fact that the thing we call love does not last forever. This does not mean that marriages break up. Things like the convenience of living under the same roof, the sheer comfort that people draw from just having another person around, keeps them together. I would say that this "lovelessness", pardon me for using such a terrible word, set in rather early in their marriage.'

Sohini persists, wants to know more.

'I would go as far as to say that they married for the wrong reasons, reasons other than mutual attraction.'

What Sohini gathers from Ahin Mitra's convoluted account is that, for Ronen, Nayantara was the quintessence of a trophy wife with her northern, convent-honed sophistication, lack of personal ambition and a fertile womb. She seemed content with volunteering for charities, organizing lavish parties, achieving a perfect layer of meringue on top of her signature dessert and participating enthusiastically in the welfare programmes for the Dubash Industries workers.

Nonnie had made peace with this utilitarian arrangement of their marriage right from the beginning. She had her reasons. For her the marriage was primarily a sanctuary from the sadness of her existence in Delhi with her emotionally absent mother and a father who worked hard at his clinic and harder still to see the smallest sign of joy in his wife. She was apparently close to her father, a slightly absent-minded man fond of Urdu poetry who died when she was thirty-two. Her mother passed away a year later. Nonnie had severe conflicts with her children that seemed to have escalated with the onset of Ahona's adolescence. In this conflict they were an unfairly divided house with Ronen taking the children's side, three pitted against one.

# 7

# Contemplation

An army of stray cats has invaded Arjun's neighbourhood. He sees them in the morning, the fat tabbies basking on the ledges in the sun, the kittens gambolling on the pavement or snarling at each other in their mock fights and the more enterprising scavengers perched precariously on the edges of the communal garbage bins. He knows very little about feline behaviour but, from their piercing howls at night, he conjectures that it is their mating season.

Tonight his body is so fatigued that he thinks he can sleep standing up with his eyes open. But when he finally lies down, his wired mind will not let him sleep. The cats begin their nocturnal ritual, a low mewling building up to an atonal chorus of howls and shrieks. He thinks their cries are louder tonight, a pervasive desperation in their mating calls. Or perhaps his frayed nerves have made him more alert, his brain more alive to a larger spectrum of frequencies. He wishes Bonani was lying next to him. He needs to talk, to unload the burden of information that sits on his brain.

He could rely on her schoolteacher patience to listen to his theories and hypotheses as if she was the investigator, not him. But his wife has been dead for eight years now, felled by a truck in front of their house, dead on the spot, dead in the split of a second even before the screech of the braking tyres had time to die down.

As he thinks about the events of the last two days, he wonders what he has found most unsettling. He was not perturbed by Nayantara's outburst. He was a case officer in the murder of a seven-year-old child and the grisly accidents of two teenagers, and remembers their parents screaming and clawing at each other in a raw and unwinnable fight of blame. He believes that for the parents of a dead child, blaming the other is the only vent available to release the impotence of sorrow.

His mind is, however, dwelling on Shonjoy. In Arjun's naive philosophy, grief is not simple sorrow or dookkho, the Bengali word that comes to his mind in these musings. Dookkho fuses with other emotions to produce a more complex compound called grief. He is an only child and does not understand the emotions that bond siblings. However, he believes that what he has seen in

Shonjoy is not pure dookkho. There is another element, a dominant emotion, combined with it. He wonders if it could be guilt.

—

Sohini has made peace with her years of insomnia. She is sitting in her burgundy armchair, has popped two pills of high dosage Alprazolam that she hopes will calm her frayed mind and is pouring herself a vodka. She uses her fingers to measure the amount she has poured, a charade that she goes through to ration her alcohol intake. She always resolves to stop at two and then allows herself another finger and then another.

Her apprehensions run deep: she suspects that as in the Vivek Sethia case she is being drawn into a game whose rules she, as a lowly pawn, does not understand. She is not particularly intrigued by Shonjoy's state of mind. A visit to any of the city's morgues – the poor air conditioning impotent against the march of decay of body tissues, the putrid stench of this decay permeating every pore and surface it encounters, the sight of the bodies lying in the corridor with the occasional stray dog in search of a meal sniffing at a dead foot or hand slipped out from under the white sheets that cover them – has the power to unhinge the mind. Then there is the process of identifying the body, hastily stitched together like a torn pair of sandals, after the pathologist's examination. It is difficult, she knows, to accept this flagrant degradation of death.

Investigators develop an individual process of enquiry, a pattern of thinking that he or she tends to repeat. Sohini's mind works on a hunch, an instinct whose roots she has never been able to trace. She builds on it, finding connections, unearthing evidence, giving it flesh and bones in the hope of telling a story that will stand up in a court of law. She finds this overt dependence on her gut a deep flaw in herself that she promises to erase each time she begins a probe – to think out of the box that her mind is trapped in. It is not that easy. Her way of building a case is so deeply embedded in her mind, so unshakeable a gestalt, that she finds herself returning to it again and again.

Her mind keeps going back to Nayantara's outburst at her interview, especially the words spoken as her anger ebbed. 'You know very well that's not the only thing I am blaming you for, Ronen…' What other blame did Ronen have to shoulder? Sohini's instinct tells her that the Chatterjees know much more about Ahona's death than they have bothered to tell her. Did they have a hand in the killing as well, she wonders.

---

DCM is a creature of habit and always drinks a post-dinner double peg of dark Old Monk rum on his small balcony where he also smokes his day's second cigarette. The half glass of water that he mixes with the rum gives it the colour of honey.

Something bothers him about the way the Chatterjee girl has been killed. It does not have the deranged brutality of a crime of passion nor the quick efficiency of a professional killing. There seems to be a deliberate slowness about this killing, a languor almost, in the way the killer trussed up the victim, gagged her, placed her in a position of his choice and then severed her head.

Was it a ritual of some sort? His mind races back twenty years to the only ritual killing he has investigated. Eight young girls had been beheaded within a span of eight years, all part of a ritual, human sacrifices by a deranged tantric priest to appease a goddess. Those killings too had had the same sense of unhurriedness, a pacing out, a calibrated choreography of death. The symbols of ritual were more overt in those deaths – the marigolds, the sticks of cloying incense and the vermilion streak. Perhaps there were symbols in this killing too that they have missed, totems and rites of an unknown faith.

DCM has also noted a precision in the way the murder weapon has been used, a perfect identification of the sweet spot on her neck aimed to maximize the force of the blow. The image of an elegant on-drive by a seasoned cricketer appears in his mind's eye, the sheer beauty of the arc of the willow, the musical roundness of the thwack as the heart of the bat connects with leather. Words follow this image – 'skill' and 'practice'. Questions come in their wake. Where did he learn his craft? How did he hone it? Were there others whose napes he had brought his weapon down on to master this skill?

He wonders if he should share these musings with Sohini but decides against it. Of late, his ability to make these quick leaps of deduction and swiftly construct a hypothesis has been attracting too many critics for his comfort, critics who also happened to be in positions of power. Sukesh Shastri, the new assistant commissioner at the crime branch, has complained to the commissioner about him for botching up an obvious dowry death with his testimony in court.

'Stick to forensics, Durgababu,' the commissioner had admonished. 'Don't get into the business of fairy tales.'

DCM wanted to tell him that it was the principles of forensic enquiry that had led him to his conclusions but had refrained. His contract was due to expire in nine months and he would rather avoid confrontation.

# 8

# The Press

The press has been reporting on the murder relentlessly. A 'high society' crime, as television anchors have described it, is rare. In the Darwinian world of the Bengali media, the failure of a channel or paper to exploit it and climb up in viewer or readership surveys could mean a sharp drop in advertising revenues, the lifeblood of its species. The initial reportage, begun on the afternoon after the murder, has been factual and objective except for the fact that all the television channels have described their own report as an 'exclusive' newsbreak.

The police have cordoned off Ahona's flat and the television cameramen have had little to do except experiment with different angles in shooting the building's exterior. While most of the television companies have sent their veterans, there are fresh-faced rookies as well who are both excited and nervous at covering their first murder. They break into smiles at the most inappropriate moments of their breathy spiels much to the chagrin of their producers. The cameramen concur that the small iron gate at the entrance provides the most interesting backdrop and constant jostling for standing room there has led to frayed nerves. Small fights are breaking out.

With the interiors of the flat out of bounds for the camera's prying lenses and very few substantive facts about the murder known to the press, the first day's visuals have been bland, largely varied shots of the exterior of Ahona's house played in a continuous loop, the bewildered face of Mrs Talukdar's nurse clearly visible in the upstairs window. These have been interspersed with some stills of Ronen Chatterjee, excavated from their archives, addressing an audience at a Rotary club event on corporate social responsibility. An enterprising channel has extracted a photograph of Ahona from her Facebook page but this has led to an uproar in the social media about the victim's privacy. The channel's response has been to pixelate part of her face, leaving the chin and forehead untouched.

The visuals and the repetitive reportage on the bare facts of the murder are punctuated with some terse interviews. Some of the neighbourhood guards have been persuaded to speak but they are wary and say very little except to deny that they saw or know anything related to the crime. Some of the onlookers, visibly excited to be on live television, are more enthusiastic and some even offer their own theories about the murder. This is, however, discouraged and the reporters want to stick to their script of harmless questions like 'What do you feel about the rise in crime in the city?' or 'Do you fear for the safety of your children?' The answers are predictably indignant and full of rant against the government and the police.

The police held a press conference at their headquarters but that has not satisfied the reporters. Deputy Commissioner Dipayan Mukherjee fended off most of the questions with a terse 'We'll let you know,' and that, somewhat predictably, earned him the sobriquet 'DC let-you-know' in the tabloids. He has also refused to divulge who was leading the probe into this ghastly crime.

'As of now, I am in charge of the case. We will let you know if there are any more developments.'

The top echelons of the police realize that Sohini's sudden return to the crime branch and her assignment to this case are likely to add another twist to this mystery. They want to hold off on the announcement until they can come up with a credible story.

The next day sees a sharp turn in the flow of events. Someone, either from the local police station or, as Arjun suspects, the forensic pathologist's team, has leaked the fact that the murder was a decapitation. The news reports suddenly become more opinionated and speculative. Camera shots are punctuated with amateurish and decidedly tasteless animations, professing to provide a 'dramatic recreation' of the murder.

One channel in a bid to stand out even features a guillotine with its slanted blade moving down at a regular frequency and then rising after a brief hiatus dripping with blood. A high-pitched theatricality has begun to creep into the coverage, which reminds him of the actors in Bengali folk theatre, the jatra, with their dialogues building up to a crescendo and the crashing fall to a dramatic whisper.

In the evening, the talk shows begin. Each channel has an army of experts who offer their views on a range of things related to the murder. There is general lament about the lack of safety in the city, an inconclusive discussion on the motive behind the murder while psychologists try to piece together a profile of the murderer based on his grisly choice of method. Their observations, however, are remarkably banal.

The anchor on Aaro Chobbish (Another Twenty-four), an up-and-coming channel known for its edgy reporting, wants to know from Tapash Mitra, one of the city's top psychiatrists, why crimes are getting increasingly violent in the city.

Mitra decides to answer in broad generalities. 'Well, the pressures of city life are mounting as things get more and more competitive. There is a lot of repressed stress, undiagnosed psychological pathologies that could culminate in this sort of violence.'

The anchor is not satisfied. She wants more categorical

assertions and tight theories. In the seven minutes of airtime that her producer has allotted Dr Mitra, she wants a perfect sketch of the killer's psyche. Three of these seven minutes are up and she does not wish to waste the other four. She bombards him with a set of questions.

'Are you suggesting that this was the work of a psychopath?' she asks him. 'Could this be a serial killer? Do you think the sense of dislocation that migrant workers face in an alien city is a factor in the rise in these brutal crimes?'

'You have asked me a lot of questions,' Dr Mitra replies with a trace of irritation in his voice, 'and you are clearly trying to put words in my mouth. What you are suggesting is theoretically possible but you must realize that as a medical professional it would be irresponsible and unethical on my part to jump to any definite conclusion.'

The conservatives, mostly retired police officers and politicians from the ruling party in government, bring up the issue of the parents' apparent callousness in allowing a young woman to live on her own. Ambarish Ghosh, three-time Member of Parliament, now in his seventies, turns apoplectic on the Ajker Bangla (Today's Bengal) channel. 'What kind of society do we live in where parents allow their young daughters this kind of independence? The parents have to take part of the blame for this murder,' he demands.

However, Ghosh and others of his persuasion face the self-righteous wrath of the feminists on the panels and the opposition politicians who blame the government for its insensitivity to the rights of women.

As she flips through these channels with her television's remote control, Sohini's finger stops at a channel where a young politician, Tarok Panda, is speaking. He is what the media calls a 'young Turk', an articulate opposition member of the state legislature who, despite his youth and the fact that his constituency is largely rural, has become an official party spokesman.

'We have to explore all angles in this murder. It is common knowledge that Dubash Industries and the government had fallen out over the decision to open the purchase of construction equipment to e-tendering. Sources tell me that the Public Works Department minister and Ronenbabu had a vicious spat over this. Please understand – I am not trying to politicize this tragedy. However, we should have an open mind.'

Sohini realizes that the 'politicization' that Ronen Chatterjee so dreads has entered the bullpen.

---

Sohini usually reads an English daily that she carries with her to work. She is a late riser and the sliver of morning spent at home is too rushed to even skim through the headlines. She is comfortable reading in her car and if she finds something interesting she saves it for the office. It fills a part of her morning as she commences her struggle to get through her workless days. However, as her new investigation has begun she has asked the paperboy to deliver a heap of Bengali newspapers.

She has always liked reading their headlines – the wordsmiths at the Bengali dailies have both a way with words and a sardonic wit that can turn the most banal into the titillating. These craftsmen of the copydesk do not disappoint her with their pithy one-line captions that anchor the reports of Ahona's murder. The only artistes in the drab world of facts, they tread the thin line between provocation and offensiveness with the finesse of a seasoned tightrope walker.

The papers are also a mine of information on trivia surrounding the case – they tell Sohini that Ahona won a prize for English literature in school, of a minor role in a production of *A Midsummer Night's Dream* in college, her expertise at badminton and so forth. All this is gleaned from her friends and teachers that their reporters manage to speak to before the police.

On the second day of the investigation, as she unfurls the roll of papers that are flung with practised skill into her balcony, a glance at a headline in one newspaper, *Aaj Porjonto* (Until Today), induces the kind of deep dread that she had last experienced in the dying days of the Swati Mukherjee strangulation case that marked her descent into professional obscurity. It is an intensely physical fear that in a second sends a rush of adrenaline into her veins so strong that she feels dizzy, stumbles and has to seek the support of the wall.

The headline in Bengali that screams in her face roughly translated reads 'Junkie Alcoholic Asked to Lead Murder Probe'. The story that follows has some facts right – her regular disappearance in the middle of the day and the symptoms of over-medication and alcohol abuse she displays are reported correctly. There is a sketchy account of her fall from grace but she is made out to be a rogue cop on the payroll of the rivals of the family whose scion she had tried to frame. There are gross distortions of the truth as well. Her dependence on tranquillizers is reported as an addiction to cocaine. Cocaine is available in the city and is the drug of choice of the affluent. It is, however, expensive and not a habit that a police officer's salary can support. Thus the accusation carries with it the added insinuation of possible connivance with the dealers of the drug or a secret payout for an illicit favour.

She is also reported to carry a thermos of alcohol with her and like Winston Churchill in his black dog days sip at it through her abbreviated workday. All this is attributed to unnamed sources in both the crime branch and the civil defence department.

Subhendubabu calls on her cellphone. He dispenses with pleasantries and asks, 'Is any of this true?'

All Sohini can say is, 'I have never even seen cocaine, let alone used it, and I don't drink in the office.'

'Continue with the investigation and I will get back to you after speaking to CM saheb.'

There are a number of calls from Ronen that she ignores. However, she responds to Arjun at the first ring of her phone. He does not mention the news report and asks for instructions. She tells him that they need to finish their pending interviews.

# 9

# Withdrawal Symptoms

He has always had the intense watchfulness of a hunting animal monitoring his prey. As a child he was admonished for his steady stare at unfamiliar visitors to his home and his refusal to turn his gaze away. He has heard hushed whispers among his peers at school and college that they found his stare unnerving, a madman's stare they called it. In his current profession, this watchfulness helps as it is construed as attentiveness. Those who share their woes, their anger and disappointments with him like the fact that his focus never seems to waver from them.

But in the days that follow a kill he falters. He is restive and unable to concentrate. His body is assailed by a heroin addict's itch, as if there are a thousand insects crawling all over, maggots in his brain gnawing away at its grey softness. These are withdrawal symptoms that he has to endure in the hope his brain will stamp them out soon. If they do not subside, the only cure is for him to kill again.

It is too soon. He needs to be cautious, to watch carefully and plan his next move. He has taken a few days off from work afraid that he might reveal this side of himself, a side that his colleagues have never seen – so stark in its contrast to the solicitous yet detached professional calmness they are used to.

He sits down on his rocking chair, opens his bag, fishes out a syringe and unwraps a disposable needle from its sheath. The only thing that soothes him on these days of torment is morphine and he has a vial ready. It is dusk now and lamps are being switched on in the houses that he can see from his window. They don't light up together. One house follows another with pauses in between. It feels as if the city wants to hold on to the last motes of daylight that the setting sun is leaving behind.

He hates this hour, the tentativeness of this slow transition from activity to sloth. He prefers the night with the anonymity and secrecy that darkness naturally brings. He glances at his watch and stares through the window as if to will the end of this lingering dusk.

There is music coming from the small speakers that connect to his iPad port. It is an old recording of a maand sung by Kesarbai Kerkar, possibly in the forties. It is remastered from an old 78 rpm record and there is a persistent scratchiness in the sound and a nasality typical of all these old recordings. But the sheer majesty of her voice overwhelms all these flaws. He has grown up with this music – Kerkar, Barodekar, Kurdikar, Gyan Gosain, Bhismadev, Mansur – all from an era long before he was born. They bring back memories of his childhood – of an old man lying on an ornate wooden bed in a large room on the top floor of a large house, an old-fashioned Murphy record player next to him, the heaviness of the lacquer records and, most of all, the pervasive smell of piss that never leaves the room.

He injects the morphine and as it slowly lulls his body and mind he turns to the dossiers that are piled on the glass table next to him. They are labelled and stuffed with notes, newspaper clippings and the occasional photograph. They go back to a pre-computer age but this is the way he likes them. He fears the openness of the virtual world with its voyeur's prying eye. There are more mundane apprehensions – of files being unlocked or hacked from his hard drive, of cookies following every click of the computer's mouse-like, faceless spies.

These cardboard files are like his voodoo dolls and he, the shaman, can commune with their absent bodies and spirits through them. The file marked 'Ahona Chatterjee' has grown fat recently with all the newspaper clippings he has added. Perhaps he needs to get another file for her. They are always locked in an old safe inherited from his grandfather and he takes them out only when there is no fear of intrusion. He picks up a dossier and as he lifts it the lights go out. These power cuts seem to be getting more frequent these days. For a few moments he relishes the darkness that it brings but is eager to read the file that he is holding. There is a smidge of blue light coming from his iPod. He squints but finds it difficult to read the name on the cover.

# 10

# Shonjoy and Atreyi Chatterjee

Sohini and Arjun have the option of summoning their interviewees to the police headquarters but have decided against it. At this stage, it is important to make them feel at ease. A visit to the grim police building with the myths that surround it – of a torture room in the basement and a lock-up that resembles a medieval dungeon – would hardly achieve that end. Besides, the makeshift office that they have been given is an airless room on the second floor, the sole window inexplicably boarded up. It has just two chairs, two desks and a shared computer. To seat their visitors they would have to borrow a chair from one of the other offices. Sohini is reluctant to take even the smallest of favours from her new colleagues who seem visibly irked by her return.

She has always used a miniature tape recorder to record her interviews. It is not a part of police protocol and she takes the interviewees' permission to get everything on tape. It saves her the trouble of taking notes. Interviews tend to meander and contain information often not pertinent to the case. But there are snatches of conversation that open up the investigation and call for further enquiry. She plays these bits over and over again in the privacy of her office waiting for her eyebrow to reflexively rise at a sentence carelessly spoken, a pause that lingers too long or simply a sigh at an unexpected moment.

Shonjoy's interview takes place in his flat on one of the streets that connect the city's largely residential southern localities to the commercial heart of the city. Originally named after a nineteenth-century English judge, it has been renamed after an obscure Bengali poet. However, the city's deep-rooted Anglophilia has ensured that its old name has stuck.

He is much taller than his father but the sedentary life of a banker is visible in his cushioned midriff. His genes are yet to take a toll on his pate and at twenty-nine he has a full head of hair that he parts down the left. He wears glasses and behind them his eyes seem anxious. He is a different person today, more in control of himself although the devastation of the tragedy is still writ on his face.

His house reflects a blend of his and his wife's disparate tastes. It seems like a battleground for a clash of cultures – the self-confident understatement typical of 'old money' clashing with the anxious, aspirational flashiness of what

Sohini guesses comes from Atreyi's more middle-class background. Sohini likes to observe these things, get these little glimpses into the lives of the cast of characters that she will share a stage with until one of them is handcuffed and led into an airless black police van. This gives her another reason to visit their homes.

There is a large crystal chandelier in the living room that marks a strange contrast to the ethnic Indian sofa set, coffee table and the sombre teak wood display shelves that line the walls. She guesses that Atreyi has chosen most of the pieces on display – an army of gaudy ceramic dolls, multi-peeled Matryoshka dolls in a riot of peasant colours, a set of shiny crystal animals and souvenirs of the Eiffel Tower and Sydney's opera house.

—

Back at her office, Sohini winds the tape back to the sections of the interview she finds relevant.

'I am surprised that Atreyi isn't here. I don't care that she had to leave for an urgent meeting. Mr Chatterjee, this is a murder investigation and that too of your own sister. The least I expect is that your wife bothers to be around when the police visit you. The next time I need to talk to you, I'll ask you both to come to the police station.'

Shonjoy mumbles inaudibly.

Sohini attempts to diffuse the tension with a somewhat

banal question, more appropriate for a job interview than a police enquiry. 'Tell us a little bit about yourself, Mr Chatterjee.'

This innocuous query from Sohini brings out a wholly unexpected garrulousness from Shonjoy that she chooses not to interrupt. His monologue is tinged with a mix of irony, mockery and self-deprecation. She hears a sneer in his voice, a snook cocked at the rest of the world that stems from a sense of entitlement, of privilege, of a life devoid of hardship or challenges. His life seems to have followed a pattern typical of the affluent. Left largely in the care of an ayah when he was small and then the family cook when he was in his teens, his parents preoccupied with their endless parade of professional and social commitments, he had been to a missionary school run by Jesuit priests. After school hours, he was ferried regularly to the club where he learnt tennis and golf that he still plays on weekends with indifferent skill. Early evenings would be spent with one of his three tutors, finishing his homework, and then with his sister, teaching her games on the family desktop computer and, when she was older, listening to music or watching a film or an American television serial together.

He had a brief dalliance with rebellion in his first year in college that comprised essentially of smoking pot (he calls it the wicked weed, which leaves Arjun baffled), wearing Bob Marley and Che Guevara T-shirts as if it were a compulsory uniform, and growing a straggly beard. He had, however, run back to the straight and narrow by his second year, giving in to pressure from both his peers and his father to build his career.

A middling student in school and college, he cleared the notoriously difficult entrance test for the country's business schools and surprisingly found a place at an institute somewhere at the top of the pecking order. Atreyi was a classmate, an ambitious and gritty middle-class girl from a small town in the north of the state.

They were hired from campus by the same bank, a largish multinational keen to increase its presence in the East. Their knowledge of Bengali was seen as an asset by the bank, which was lowering its sights from the super-affluent to the less rich but aspirational (a word that had been drummed into their heads at many training sessions) middle classes. After a year she had switched to another bank.

'You were very close to Ahona. Why do you think she was so depressed?' Sohini asks.

'I don't think there was one single reason. She did feel neglected by our parents and resentful towards them. It was certainly more than typical adolescent rebelliousness. However, from whatever little I understand of the subject, new research shows that it is largely a chemical imbalance in the brain that causes depression. It is also hereditary. Did my mother mention that my grandmother was depressive?'

'Yes, she did,' Sohini replies. 'Mr Chatterjee, your call records show that you rang your sister every evening. The duration of the calls went up suddenly over the last two months. Was there any reason for this?'

Shonjoy replies, 'As you know she was emotionally disturbed and I was possibly the person closest to her. So I called her every evening to make sure she was okay, whether Maya was staying the night, whether she had taken her medication and so forth. The calls got longer because Ahona was terribly upset by Baba's decision to sell a small farmhouse that we own about a hundred kilometres north of the city. I shouldn't call it a farmhouse really – it's more a cottage with about three bighas of land. Ahona liked it because it was right next to the river. She was trying to dissuade Baba, even threatening to sue him though she hardly had a case. I discussed this with her regularly and tried to calm her down.'

'Was Atreyi aware of these calls?'

Shonjoy sounds irritated by this question. 'I think this is a private matter and has little to do with a murder investigation. However, since you ask, let me make it clear that Atreyi was not fond of my sister and resented my closeness to her. I tried to make sure that she wasn't around when I called Ahona. But if she had checked my phone, she would have known that I called her often.'

Then Arjun's voice is heard for the first time in the conversation. 'Shonjoybabu, I know this might sound a little strange but can you think of anyone who would want to harm your sister?'

Shonjoy answers after a moment. 'Now that I think about

it, there was that silly incident with Raju, a temporary driver I had about four months back. Ahona used taxis to get to work and back but occasionally when she went out in the evening I insisted that she take my car. Raju turned out to be rather too fond of the bottle. He had driven Ahona down that evening to the Goethe Institut for a concert. While she was at the concert, he got dead drunk and forgot to pick her up. I sent him over to her flat the next morning to apologize and they had a vicious row. He threatened to kill her and even claimed to have a weapon – I think it was a cleaver of sorts – that he would use on her. Of course, I sacked him immediately but dismissed his threat as an alcoholic's rant, nothing more.'

'Mr Chatterjee, I would like to meet your wife this evening. I will do you the courtesy of not asking her to come to the police headquarters. We will be back at seven in the evening. Please ensure that she is here. And incidentally, we would like to talk to her alone.'

Sohini switches off the recorder.

---

Atreyi Chatterjee is an attractive woman, a head-turner. Sohini has to try hard to suppress a smile when she sees the expression on Arjun's face as she walks into the living room. Her personal style is a far cry from the gaudiness of her home decor. Clad in a simple but expensive cotton sari and with minimal make-up, she has the understated gloss of high-end fashion magazines. She has just returned from work and, although she has clearly been briefed by Shonjoy about their visit, looks annoyed by their intrusion.

She speaks only in English, the badge of the upwardly mobile professional class. There are distinct traces of a provincial education – her vowels are curtailed or elongated in the wrong places.

Sohini decides to take an aggressive approach in her questioning. 'I am sorry to put it like this but you don't seem too affected by Ahona's death,' Sohini says.

'Everyone in the family knows that I wasn't particularly fond of her. Of course, I didn't wish her dead but I cannot bring myself to grieve for her.'

'May I ask why?'

'I thought she was a spoilt brat who got away with all her tantrums. She was twenty-two but she behaved like a thirteen-year-old when she wanted her way with things. I come from a small-town, middle-class family. I have been brought up with a completely different set of values.'

'Your husband was apparently very fond of her.'

'Fond? He was obsessed with her, treated her like a baby. I know he spent half his evening talking to her, and he visited her regularly. I think he was responsible for her never quite growing up. I have two brothers I am close to but our relationship is nothing like this. This was abnormal. I know she was diagnosed as clinically depressed but she used her disease as a shield to keep responsibilities away.'

'What about your in-laws?'

'Quite honestly, I have never quite fathomed my mother-in-law. The life and soul of the lavish parties they throw, but otherwise so distanced from her children. My father-in-law is a kind, jovial person but he was also terribly obsessed with Ahona.'

'You were in Mumbai the night of the murder. When did you come back?'

'Shonjoy called the next morning, right after the body was discovered and the police informed the family. He was hysterical. I was scheduled to come back in the evening but I cancelled my afternoon meeting and rushed back on an eleven o'clock flight.'

'Thank you for sparing time. I know it's an intrusion but you must understand that we are conducting a murder investigation. We might need to call you or meet you again.'

'That's all right. Will you wait a moment? I will get you my business card.'

---

Arjun hasn't brought his car today and Sohini is dropping him home. The madness of the rush hour has subsided and the streets are relatively empty. Arjun and Sohini are both silent, lost in their thoughts. Ram Bahadur tries to make conversation with Sohini. She rebuffs him and repents immediately but does not apologize.

She thinks of Shonjoy and Ahona's relationship, his 'abnormal' obsession with her as Atreyi described it. She has heard of overprotective older siblings: her mother has often complained to her that Tintu, her cousin, was more like a doting father to his sister Mita than a brother. She was only four years younger. But was there something more to the Shonjoy and Ahona relationship than a deep sibling bond? Why was Nayantara a bad mother, so detached from her children? Was she also depressed like her mother, and her daughter? Did Ronen try to compensate for this by always taking their side or was there some other reason?

A strange thought has entered Arjun's mind, an irrational suspicion based neither on fact nor deduction. He tries very hard to shake it off but it continues to haunt him as he alights from the car in front of the narrow lane where his house is located and thanks both Sohini and Ram Bahadur. He is convinced that Shonjoy is capable of extreme violence.

# 11

# Sniper Attack

The media attack on Sohini is not a continuous barrage of artillery. Instead, she finds herself in the unwavering gunsight of a lone sniper who shoots to wound rather than to kill. The 'scoop' is exclusive in the correct dictionary sense of the word in that it is led by a single newspaper – *Aaj Porjonto* – and its sister television channel. The so-called exposé has now gone beyond her alcoholism and drug abuse, and has turned both vicious and increasingly creative in its fabrications about her personal and professional life. There are allegations of her links with the drug mafia in the district of her first posting that has become a key player in the conduit of drugs from Burma. There are also hints of sexual favours granted in her initial days in police to climb up the professional ladder.

Some of *Aaj Porjonto*'s competitors are sulking for having

missed this scoop, that the deep-throat has preferred their competitor over them. They confine themselves to reportage of the murder. Some papers have more explicitly taken her side. There had been a degree of public outrage when she was suddenly dropped from the infamous Swati Mukherjee case and a number of them had run a campaign in her support. They try to rekindle memories of the five-year-old case and suggest that an upright police officer has finally got justice.

This could be genuine empathy for Sohini but the cynics suggest that this is a way of countering *Aaj Porjonto*'s sudden spike in readership after l'affaire Sohini. However, a five-year-old episode is ancient history in a world of shrinking attention spans and memories. *Aaj Porjonto* is getting the upper hand.

The paper is owned by Archishman Basu. He is not just the publisher but plays a role on the editorial desk penning a vitriolic daily column on what he terms the 'burning issue' of the day. The daily is a hundred years old and was started by Abinash Chandra Deb to espouse the cause of militant resistance to British rule and openly lampoon the rising ideology of passive non-violence. Although it was a Bengali daily, it originally went by the name of *Bengal Mail*.

The paper went through a period of decline in the seventies and eighties when Abinash's son Amiyo, a shy, retiring man, tried to run it. Archishman took over the paper in the early nineties. His antecedents were the subject of much speculation and he made no effort to dispel them.

The accepted thesis was that the Basu family came from a northern district that flanked Bangladesh. Their wealth was rumoured to be trade, both licit and illicit, across the two borders. There were also some hard, indisputable facts. The Basu family owned a small Dornier aircraft; Archishman had a degree from an American liberal arts college; he had interned with a small mid-western television channel as a reporter.

When he took over the *Bengal Mail* the first task that he set for himself was to rename the paper. The stodgy *Bengal Mail* became *Aaj Porjonto*, positioned as a paper that focused on gritty investigative pieces but largely on local issues, leaving the big national news stories to the other papers. The tagline below the masthead roughly translated to 'Our news is the nation's news'.

Archishman carefully constructed a persona for himself – that of a stylish and slightly eccentric activist publisher-editor. The paper justified its popularity by doing some well-researched investigative pieces. A series of stories on the pollution of the city's groundwater by its tanners and the complex mesh of payoffs to the municipal authorities won the paper a national award.

In the late nineties, Archishman started a television channel with news during the day and evenings devoted to investigative features, documentaries and a talk show. This was lauded as a pioneering step that would usher in a media revolution.

Audience preference changed and competition increased as the investment needed to start a television channel or float a paper dipped. Official statistics might show the state as poor but it is known to be cash-rich and this cash is always seeking legitimacy. Ownership of a newspaper or television channel offered this. By the late noughties both Basu's channel and the newspaper were floundering.

To lift its sagging fortunes Archishman discovered a new niche – investigative stories that sought out the prurient and salacious in the city's underbelly. This included long features on the proliferation of prostitutes in the plush hotels, the rise in male streetwalkers in the leafy surroundings of the man-made lakes in the southern neighbourhoods or the sexual favours sought by a high court judge for friendly judgements.

Archishman's ally in this was Shubhro Roy, host of the talk show *An Hour with Shubhro*. Often dressed entirely in black like a nightclub bouncer, he combined the hectoring style of a Bible belt preacher with a careful disregard for the politically correct that he learnt from watching videos of American right-wing television channels.

Media analysts note a spike in viewership in the last five minutes of his show. This is the moment he faces the camera and offers a brief summation of the show. It is more a short sermon. In the dying minutes of the show just before the credits start scrolling, he leaves his audience with a set of questions to ponder over.

The episode on Sohini ended with the following questions:

'Am I right in assuming that the police is the upholder of the law of the land? Am I also correct in assuming that the consumption of drugs is against the law? Is it irrational for me to hypothesize that someone who consumes these drugs will protect the purveyors of these drugs? Would I be wrong in assuming that the only reason for assigning a sensitive case to a known alcoholic and drug addict could only be a fiendish political conspiracy? Goodnight, nomoshkar.'

The rise in viewer ratings and circulation was reason enough for Basu and Roy to step up their campaign against Sohini. But that is perhaps not all. If one is patient enough to trawl through *Aaj Porjonto*'s balance sheet, there is an entry likely to grab attention. It shows an outstanding ten-crore-rupee loan taken from Sethia Industries whose current deputy managing director Sohini had once tried to arrest.

# 12

# Saikat Bhattacharya

Saikat's institute is on the eastern outskirts of the city. It is a new campus, funded by the central government, but has quickly fallen into a state of dishabille that academics seem to thrive in. The walls are painted with cheap whitewash that is not quite white but a weak powder blue. It has peeled in places exposing concrete and occasionally brickwork. There is a large lawn in front that is overgrown with weeds and the flower beds function as a communal ashtray.

Sohini and Arjun have come here after a visit to Ahona's office. Her boss Soumen and two other colleagues they interviewed were eager to help but offered no real insight. She had worked at the publishing house for barely a year, was a competent worker but uninterested in her colleagues and extremely guarded about herself.

He is a senior fellow close to completing his doctoral

thesis and has a tiny office on the third floor. The furniture is standard government issue – a steel almirah, a shelf overflowing with books, a wooden desk and two mismatched chairs. Saikat is clad in the unmistakable uniform of his trade – a khadi kurta, unwashed baggy jeans and leather slippers. He wears glasses and has a thick beard that somehow seems incongruous on his lean face. He has a distracted air about him that Sohini at first glance thinks is carefully cultivated to conform to the stereotype of the absent-minded academic.

'Shonjoy told me that you were in the US for a PhD but you came back after two years. Why?' Sohini asks.

'It's a long story. I had gone with a couple of friends to Mexico on our spring break. I caught a particularly vicious strain of tuberculosis there and spent eight weeks in my university hospital. I needed to recuperate and came home. This institute is very good, the PhD is internationally recognized and some of the faculty members are regarded as really top class in their field. I saw no reason to go back to the US to get a doctorate.'

'How did you meet Ahona?'

'A friend, Urmi, introduced us at the Hitchcock retrospective last November. We discovered we had common interests and stayed in touch. You could call it a relationship of sorts.'

'Why did you end it?'

'Look, I could give you a bogus answer but I'm going to be honest. I believe that any adult relationship has to have a physical aspect. Ahona was just not interested in sex. In fact, she seemed traumatized by the couple of attempts I made to, well, make love. I was aware that she was a depressive. Maybe the drugs did this to her. I couldn't handle it and put an end to it in February.'

'How did she take it?'

'She was surprisingly calm. Didn't break down or anything. She seemed to understand what I told her. But we didn't stay friends. I've had no contact with her ever since. She didn't call me either. I was of course shocked to hear of her murder. But again I'll be dead honest with you. It was a brief affair and I haven't exactly been devastated. Nonetheless I must confess that the fact that someone I knew so closely has been killed so brutally gives me the creeps.'

'Thank you for being so candid.'

'Let me ask you a routine question,' interrupts Arjun. 'Where were you between eight and eleven on the evening of Ahona's death?'

'This seems straight out of a detective novel.' Saikat makes a weak attempt at humour. 'I usually stay fairly late at the institute and work in the computer lab. I have the regular stuff like MATLAB on my laptop but I need some specialized software for my research that only the lab computers have. I was at the institute at the time. As a senior fellow, I am entitled to a key and lock up if I am the last to leave. The lab was fairly empty that evening but I am sure that some postgrads were around. I don't quite remember their faces but if you ask around you will come across someone who saw me.'

Sohini switches off the tape recorder.

In her early days at the crime branch, Sohini had a mentor, Deputy Commissioner Umesh Bose. She still remembers being summoned to his office after she had submitted a case file. 'Ms Sen,' Bose had said, 'you have a terrible habit. You take a witness's testimony as gospel truth. That is the worst mistake you can make as an investigator. Please cross-check your facts and evidence. Being gullible is a crime in this force.' Sohini has not forgotten this admonishment, delivered in Bose's perennially irritated bark. She will verify Saikat's statements.

Arjun has noted down the name of his American university. It turns out to be a massive state university on the eastern seaboard with large engineering and mathematics departments, a hive for Indian and East Asian students. Sohini sends an email to the head of the mathematics department, a Professor G.V. Karthikeyan, asking if she could speak to him about Saikat.

The reply comes a good seven hours later given the difference in time. Karthikeyan claims to have known Saikat well and would be happy to Skype with her.

She is barely comfortable with using her email account and has never used Skype before. She calls Brinda, who patiently takes her through the installation of the software. The interview takes place late in the evening for Sohini and early morning for the professor.

Karthikeyan was Saikat's faculty mentor for a year and remembers him very well. The resolution of her screen is poor and all she can make out is that he is dark, wears glasses and is clad in a white shirt. He does most of the talking, in a measured voice that bears traces of his Tamil origins overlaid with an American twang.

'Saikat was mediocre by the standards we expect in American academia, a plodder who had delusions that he could do top rate theory. He tried to dabble in an overcrowded field like string theory and failed miserably. We asked him to do something more applied, perhaps jointly with the engineering school. But that hurt his inflated Bengali ego. He developed a deep sense of paranoia by the time he was in his third semester.'

---

Saikat leaves Lowes Hall where the mathematics department is located. He has just seen his grade for the individual project assessment. He has a B minus. There is only one A grade and that has gone to Soosung Jong, his flatmate in the first semester. He is headed towards the student union where he will buy an egg salad sandwich and a cup of coffee from the co-op in the basement. He crosses the parking lot when he sees Soosung drive in, park his white Jetta and get off. He seems headed for Lowes

Hall. Saikat suddenly breaks into a little jog towards him. Soosung is as usual dressed somewhat formally in a black blazer and pressed khaki chinos. Saikat is now close to him. Soosung recognizes him in the light of the halogen lamp, raises his hand and says, 'Hey, man!'

He kicks him first in the groin and Soosung collapses to the ground with a wail. Then there is a rain of blows on the Korean's body. Saikat's kicks land but the punches often miss. When the campus police find them, an exhausted Saikat is found lying on the ground next to Soosung's seemingly lifeless body. When he is released from the lock-up after a day, he is told that his classmate had two broken ribs and a damaged spleen.

---

'You know these East Asians, Ms Sen,' Karthikeyan continues. 'They don't want to get involved with the police – Soosung didn't press charges. We had to let Saikat go and I fought hard with the rest of the faculty to give him a reference. I am happy he managed to get a place at the institute but I hope he knows that the world of math academia is a very small community. I am sure half his faculty knows what happened to him in the US. So he has to be careful about feeding the tuberculosis rubbish.

'The reason his institute puts up with him is his uncle, Chanchal Bhattacharya, who is very influential in the

Indian academic world. A member of the University Grants Commission and all that.'

Sohini thanks Karthikeyan for his help and switches off.

---

However, Sohini's tape has not recorded something that Arjun noticed. On their way out, Sohini had disappeared into the washroom for a few minutes while he lingered in front of the institute's main noticeboard. A particular notice caught his attention. It announced the death of Ambar Nath Pal, senior administrator of the computer laboratory, and offered condolences to the family on behalf of the faculty and staff. There would be a condolence meeting at the auditorium at four in the afternoon and, as a mark of respect, the computer laboratory would be closed for the rest of the day. Students and faculty had been advised in a postscript to save their work and conclude their use of other lab facilities before four as the servers would be shut down. This happened to be the day of Ahona's murder. Saikat could not have been at the laboratory that evening or night. Arjun mentions this to Sohini.

'Well done, Arjun,' Sohini tells him. 'You have the one thing that a good cop needs – a keen sense of observation.' This is her first gesture of acknowledgement that he too exists and has a role to play in this case. Arjun is not expecting this appreciation from his brooding, self-centred boss. He murmurs a quiet 'Thank you', and overcome by a bout of shyness looks out of the car window.

Saikat has climbed up their list of suspects. He has been violent in the past and is a pathological liar. An intelligent, educated man like him would also be capable of planning and executing a forensically flawless murder, the 'perfect murder' as DCM has described it. Both detectives can also think of a motive. Their layman's understanding of psychology suggests that he reacts to rejection and disappointment with a visceral rage. Thus the murder could be retribution for being sexually spurned by Ahona.

Sohini suspects that another factor is influencing their judgement. The newspapers and television channels have been reporting a mass murder on a university campus in southern United States. On a balmy Tennessee morning, a quiet Taiwanese graduate student has walked into his classroom with an automatic gun and shot six of his classmates in cold blood before shooting himself. Trawling his dorm room and the hard drive of his computer, the police had pieced together a profile that had the textbook elements of a psychopath. He had also been a PhD student in mathematics.

# 13

# The Funeral

Sohini and Arjun are at Ahona's prayer meeting, two days after she is cremated. It is not a quiet affair – Ronen and Nayantara have a large circle of friends and acquaintances. The tuberose wreaths that adorn the entrance to the Chatterjees' flat are pristine white as are the clothes that the mourners wear. Ahona's friends from college and work huddle together in one corner, sitting cross-legged on one of the mattresses that cover most of the room, covered with white sheets tarnished by faint footprints and the light dust of bare feet. The shoes form a little hill of leather and canvas close to the doorway of the vast living room. A blown-up, slightly grainy photograph of the dead woman is placed on a small podium in one side of the room.

This is not a conventional funeral. Her friends read lines of poetry or short tributes and then the singer who waits patiently by the podium will sing. As Sohini and Arjun enter, she sees a slight young woman with long hair, dressed in a white handspun ensemble, recite from Shelley's 'Adonais':

*Peace, peace! she is not dead, she doth not sleep*
*She hath awakened from the dream of life*

Sohini knows some of the lines; she has heard Orko recite this in an affected baritone in college and notices the subtle change of gender in the elegy. She sits close to the friends and in the cross-legged posture her knees hurt. She wonders if the alcohol has given her gout or if it's the onset of arthritis. Someone whispers to her that the reciter is Shefali, Ahona's childhood friend.

Shefali finishes the poem with a barely suppressed sob and sits close to Sohini. Then it's the turn of the singer, Gauri Rudra, an up-and-coming vocalist from the city's world of classical music. She has chosen a nirgun bhajan by Kabir, an abstract idea of god and yet evocative in its imagery. Sohini taps Shefali gently on the shoulder, hands her a business card and whispers, 'Can I have a quick word with you outside when this bhajan is over?'

Shefali nods her assent and they both listen to Rudra. She sings with a skill that justifies her reputation. Her voice matches the sombreness of the occasion – there is no intent to impress but only to unite the congregation in prayer, to quietly mark this solemn rite of passage.

Sohini and Shefali leave the flat and head downstairs to the lawn. There are flower beds all around and the heavy downpours of the last few months have left an air of fecundity in their wake. The plants, however, look bruised by the rain.

'I had a few questions about Ahona,' Sohini says. 'Mrs Chatterjee mentioned that you were very close to her.'

'Not any longer, although I did visit her occasionally at her flat. We grew apart in high school, around the time we took our first board exams. I am not sure what caused the rift. She had niggling bouts of illness and that affected her. She became very distant, turned away from her friends.'

'What kind of illness?' Sohini asks.

'Mostly gynaecological from what she told me. Polyps in her uterus that kept recurring, from what I remember. She had a couple of surgeries but was very secretive about them. Didn't want her friends to visit her at the hospital. She became even more withdrawn in college. We were both in the same class – English honours. She did tell me that she was on medication for clinical depression.'

'Do you know Saikat?'

'Yes, I met him a couple of times, once at her flat and the other time at a film festival. Oh yes, I must tell you about a strange incident a couple of months back. I had gone into a pharmacy to buy some medicines and I found Ahona there. I tapped her on the shoulder and when she turned around she looked very agitated. She was about to pay for the stuff she had bought but told the cashier she would take them later. Said she had left something behind in her taxi and left abruptly.'

'Did you see what she had bought?'

'No. It was all in a paper bag.'

'I must let you get back to the prayer meeting. Mrs Chatterjee gave me your number. I hope you won't mind if I call in case I have any other questions.'

'Of course not.'

As Sohini walks towards the porch, Arjun comes forward and tells her that there is a man waiting to speak to her. He is sitting on a bench some distance away, smoking a cigarette, and when he sees her approaching, he stubs it out and walks towards her.

'Ms Sen, I am Sandip Chakraborty, Ahona's psychiatrist. I was wondering if I could have a few minutes of your time.'

He is tall and looks fit in the loose-limbed way of people who play a sport regularly. He is remarkably fair, the kind of fairness she associates with children of old landowning families, the legacy of brides chosen for generations on the sole criterion of their complexion. His perfect shave, his haircut, skin tone and manicure speak of expensive grooming. From the salt and pepper of his hair, the slight fleshiness of his face and the bifocal spectacles that hang from a delicate silver chain around his neck she guesses that he is about her age or a couple of years younger.

'Dr Chakraborty, I'd be more than happy to spare a few

minutes now. But I'd prefer to have more of your time. Could I see you perhaps at your clinic this evening? I could stop by after you are done with your patients.'

'I won't be at the clinic this evening and have a couple of pressing commitments. But tomorrow is perfect if that suits you. I start my clinic at four and usually wind up by eight.' He fishes out his visiting card from his wallet and hands it to Sohini.

# 14

# Maya Sikdar

Maya was married to Kanai Sikdar when she was seventeen. She is sixty now and though he is alive and they remain married, she has hardly had the time to get to know him. Since she was fifteen, she has caught the local train at six-thirty from a far-flung suburb near the mouth of the river. The station was a good half-hour walk from her home, and that meant she had to leave her house, a curious mish-mash of brick, thatch and asbestos sheets, before six.

She started as a part-timer, a thike, a part-time maid, at different homes with different chores. She swept and swabbed at a couple, cooked at one and washed the dishes at the last households of her rounds. It would be six by the time she caught the train and after eight in the evening when she dragged her tired body home. She took the occasional Sunday off to rest her bones and catch up on sleep. Karuna, her only daughter, was born when Maya was twenty-four, a late child by the standards of her community. After she was born, her aunt, Kanai's sister, came to live with them.

Ronen has known her since she was sixteen. Except for brief absences during her marriage and childbirth she had turned up with admirable punctuality to sweep the floors. When Shonjoy was born, the Chatterjees offered her a permanent position as his nanny which entailed moving in with them. She would get a day off in the week but never on the weekend since the family entertained then.

For those like Maya and Kanai whose incomes afford just about adequate subsistence, difficult choices are made easy by the sheer force of economics. For her, moving in with the Chatterjee family meant virtually severing her ties with her small child. However, the imperatives of funding a private school for her daughter instead of abandoning her to the vagaries of the state's education system, affording medical care for an ageing mother-in-law and building a nest egg for an uncertain future found her packing her meagre belongings along with a framed photograph of her child and seamlessly entering the Chatterjee household. She has stayed with them since, a member of the household, a trusted serf but never part of the family.

---

Sohini and Arjun meet her at the small private nursing home

close to the Chatterjee residence. The reception promises a certain kind of opulence inside, at least a quiet efficiency that being 'private' signifies in this country. But on walking past the reception, they find that it suddenly degenerates into the kind of disorderliness associated with government hospitals. Truant nurses are being summoned both by patients and by doctors, heart and lung machines are left unmonitored, the corridors need a swab and the rubbish bins overflow with piles of used surgical bandages, syringes and empty medicine vials.

Maya is in a single room and the effect of heavy sedatives hasn't worn off. She had been at her daughter's house on the night of the murder, following her usual arrangement with Ahona, and had returned the morning after at eight-thirty (Ahona was a late riser). After ringing the bell frantically for a few minutes, she had fished out her own set of keys and unlocked the door. On finding the body, she had broken into hysterical shrieks, attracting the neighbourhood guards, and then slumped on to the floor, unconscious.

Replaying the recorded conversation, Sohini pauses the recorder at the moments she finds important to the case.

Maya tells them that she was very close to Shonjoy and brought him up like her own child. Memsaheb, referring to Nayantara, was very busy those days. She still remains close to Shonjoy, whom she met on his regular visits to Ahona's flat.

'How often did he come?'

'At least thrice a week. Often he turned up late evening after I had left for my daughter's house. Booridīdi used to tell me he had visited.'

'Who else visited?'

'There was that gentleman with a beard who came almost every evening but that was just for three or four months. Shefalididi used to visit but of late her visits had become rare.'

'Did her parents visit at all?'

'Her father did but never memsaheb. Booridīdi went to their house occasionally on weekends.'

'Why did Ahona ask you to leave in the evenings? Weren't you supposed to stay the night?'

'She wanted to be on her own. When she set her mind on something, it was impossible to say no to her. She could get very angry if you refused her. Karuna and Deepak, my daughter and son-in-law, are very understanding. Their house is small but they always welcome me. Besides, I get a chance to spend time with Boomba, my four-year-old grandson. I never spent any time with my daughter. Now I get to spend some time with her son at least. Saheb and memsaheb are aware of this arrangement.'

She continues without any prompting. 'She was a sweet baby. I used to look after Shonjoydada, but when she was born, I was put in charge of her. Dada was six then and was happy in the company of Akram, the cook, and Pulinbabu, the driver. At that age, boys prefer to be around men.

Booridìdi was sweet but difficult, always throwing tantrums. But that is natural for a young girl. Things really changed when she turned thirteen or fourteen. She brooded a lot, fought with saheb and memsaheb all the time and became very cruel towards me. That was the time she started hurting herself, first with things like pens or a ruler. A couple of years later this graduated to blades and her small penknife. But I did not hold her cruelty against her. I knew – memsaheb told me – that she had an illness of the head. You can't hold a grudge against someone who is ill.'

'I was surprised that we did not find any medicines in the house. Do you know why?' Sohini asks.

'This is a new obsession that didi had – hiding her medicines,' Maya replies. 'It started about two months ago. God knows why. You will find them in one of the condiment boxes in the kitchen but you have to look really carefully.'

Sohini wants Maya to tell her a little more about Shonjoy, to go beyond the platitudes she has used to describe the man who was once her ward, her proxy child. She believes that Shonjoy's eagerness to talk about himself so candidly was an attempt to build a facade and she wants to know what lies behind it.

Sohini senses Maya's fierce loyalty to the Chatterjees and she knows that she must use her skills as a seasoned interrogator to scale the wall of silence that this loyalty is likely to create. She does not have even the shred of a case against Maya, not the slightest reason to justify taking her into police custody. Thus she must leverage this barely educated woman's gullibility and her deeply ingrained fear of the police to get her answers.

She tells Maya gently, 'We are investigating a murder, Maya. If you don't tell us everything, we will be forced to take you to the station and perhaps keep you there for a few nights. It is not up to me. I know you have nothing to do with all this. But unfortunately this is how the law works.'

She can see the panic on Maya's face and then the weeping starts. A nurse walks in, asks them to leave, tells them that any coercion can harm Maya. Arjun almost pushes her out of the room. Maya comes from a social class that finds it difficult to talk freely about many things. She cannot find the right words to express herself, to convey the information that she thinks will save her from incarceration. Sohini prompts her gently, often chooses a word for her to which she nods.

Shonjoy has had his share of problems. From an early age he was obsessed with sex and a compulsive masturbator. Maya has discovered him at the unlikeliest of moments playing with his engorged penis with his eyes tightly shut in the effort of conjuring up a fantasy. She has shuddered at the thought of herself being a part of these fevered imaginings. This constant need for self-gratification has frequently led him to the sleazy porn shops near the railway bridge with money stolen from his mother's bag. Akram has spotted him there. He has been caught in the net of a police raid and been slapped viciously by the officer. The slap had caused an inflammation in his ear and brought on a raging fever. In the brief spans of lucidity that punctuated his delirium, he had told her about the incident, begging her not to tell his parents.

She tells Sohini that it was common knowledge among the servants that he was also a petty shoplifter through his adolescence, filching birthday cards from a souvenir shop, CDs and DVDs from a books-and-music store in one of the city's new malls, T-shirts from a shop in the same mall and various other things. Surprisingly he hadn't been caught despite the sophisticated surveillance gadgetry that these shops have and their uniformed security guards.

An incident that haunts Maya involved their pet Labrador pup, Brutus. Shonjoy must have been around thirteen then. Brutus was teething, and had chewed up one of Shonjoy's textbooks. When Shonjoy found out, he started kicking the dog. Not satisfied with that, he ran to the kitchen, got a sharp knife and started to stab the dog. Ahona was howling. Akram tried to restrain Shonjoy but he too got stabbed in the arm. Ronen was fortunately in the house and he finally subdued Shonjoy. The dog died a few days later.

'We know that Ahona had been ill and was hospitalized a number of times. Do you know what happened?' Sohini asks.

'She had problems with her...' Maya can't find the right word and points in the direction of her pelvis. 'The strange thing was that it was saheb who did everything. Memsaheb visited her just once when she was in hospital. But that's the way she's been with the children ever since they were in their teens. When Booridi came back from the hospital, she had both a day and a night nurse and we were kept away from her.'

---

The post-mortem report has finally arrived at the police headquarters. Sohini and Arjun get a copy. The format is neat and its different sections are clearly labelled. The first comprises general observations and is followed by reports on different parts of the victim's anatomy. Section (A) is the 'head and neck'. From what they understand of the medical jargon that fills the report, the weapon entered from the back of her neck, sliced through the vertebra and the spinal cord instantaneously cutting off sensation in her body. It then sliced the internal jugulars and the carotid arteries cutting off blood supply to the brain, an event referred to as brain ischemia. But it did not penetrate beyond that and the neck muscles, the sternomastoid and thoracic muscles kept the head attached to the body.

There is a superficial wound on the skull that is likely to have caused mild and brief concussion. The pathologist has scribbled a note in the margin saying that it was possibly used to stun the victim before tying her up.

The rest of the report describes the state of her other

organs starting with the chest down to her genitals and then a somewhat isolated section on the spinal cord where the details of the injury to the spine are repeated. Ahona seems to have been healthy with no visible damage to any of her other organs. There is also no sign of sexual assault. The self-mutilation injuries are also described, though in less detail.

There is a toxicology report that notes the presence of considerable doses of selective serotonin reuptake inhibitors or antidepressants. There are no significant quantities of any other chemicals in her bloodstream. DCM has been through the report and has appended a note along with some printouts taken from the Internet.

He has taken great pains to explain that in beheadings with a single stroke, the head remains attached to the body. This does not, in his opinion, take away from the executioner's skill. The Internet articles describe decapitation of hostages by terrorist groups that is a much slower process that begins with slicing the victim's windpipe, usually with a smaller weapon. From the position of the body and the injury on the left side of Ahona's neck he has concluded that the killer was right-handed.

As Maya had predicted, a small plastic bag of medicines, concealed with a lot of care, is discovered after a long search in a tin in the kitchen cabinet that also contained turmeric, bay leaves and cardamom. The bag has in it paracetamol, some antacids, two strips of antidepressants and three strips of Vominix, a strong nausea suppressant that Sohini remembers taking for her motion sickness on her summer vacations in the hill stations of the North. The first strip is empty and there are just two tablets left in the second strip of pills. Sohini wonders why Ahona needed to hide these pills unless it was some form of compulsive disorder that had afflicted her diseased mind.

---

Durga Maity shares with Sohini his suspicion that this was not the killer's first murder but finds her response tepid. He is not offended and empathizes with her instead. For one thing, he knows he has very little to corroborate his hypothesis. Besides, the search for a psychopath entails a complete rethink of the investigation since serial killings often lack a clear textbook motive. The logical path that follows from the identification of motive also disappears. She is right, he tells himself, not to cast her net too wide.

# 15

# The Counsellor

Alpha Clinic is located in a residential neighbourhood in the city's south-east. Such clinics have mushroomed across the city over the past decade where doctors have a temporary chamber, a couple of hours in the morning or evening for a few days in the week. It calls itself 'multi-speciality', a one-stop shop for the many plaints that can afflict the human body and mind. The list of specialists outside is impressive – from the sombre oncologists and cardiac surgeons to the more lightweight cosmetic surgeons and dieticians.

They stop at the reception and ask for Sandip Chakraborty. The eager, young receptionist whose heavy make-up Sohini finds incongruous with the surroundings has many questions. Who is the patient? Have they gone through the formal registration process or would they like to fill in the form now? Was their appointment with the doctor made through the appointment desk? Do they have a reference number? Sohini loses her patience and flashes her police ID card. The questions stop, there is a faint shadow of fear on her face and she directs them to the doctor's room. The temporary nameplate that has been slipped into the holder on the door says 'S. Chakraborty, M.D. (Psych)'.

They have to wait for fifteen minutes while Dr Chakraborty sees a patient. He had given them an appointment about forty-five minutes earlier and they have missed it because of the traffic. When the patient, a young man in his twenties, leaves, the doctor himself steps out to usher them into his room.

He is solicitous, apologizing profusely for keeping them waiting. Sandip is dressed somewhat formally in a blue shirt, a light blazer and grey pants. This sartorial fastidiousness is a growing trend among the younger doctors of the city, a marked change from the doctors she saw in her childhood with their regulation attire of bush shirts and sandals.

The room has the impersonal air of a temporary office. There is a painting of Venice's Rialto bridge behind the doctor's chair and an elevated bed behind a white curtain meant for physical examination of patients. The strong smell of mouthwash and a chair with a lamp fixed to it that is now pushed to a corner suggest that the previous occupant was a dentist.

'Thank you again for meeting us. I won't keep you too long. How long was Ahona your patient?'

'Six months or so. She was Dr Sen's patient earlier but when he became a deputy director and took on a load of administrative responsibilities, he asked me to take some of his cases.'

'Dr Chakraborty...'

'Sandip, please,' he insists.

'Well, Sandip then.' Sohini continues, 'I know you might have reservations about discussing the details of your professional relationship with Ahona. And I don't know enough about psychiatry to understand some of the more technical stuff about her treatment. Or should I call it therapy? I just want to know if there was something that you learnt about her that could give us a clue about her murder.'

'I'll try to keep it simple. Her parents might have told you that she was in therapy for years. She was badly messed up. That's hardly an appropriate phrase for a psychiatrist to use but it describes her perfectly. She was dealing with a number of problems that I don't want to discuss because they are irrelevant to her murder. She was also aware that she could have inherited her illness from her grandmother and this made her all the more helpless and anxious.

'And yes,' he continues, 'I am serious about patient confidentiality and grateful that you understand my position. However, there are some things that I can discuss. Over the past few months, Ahona had become very afraid that someone would harm her, that she was in danger of some kind. We often see these episodes of paranoia among depressives. Depression and anxiety often come together and these unexplained intense fears are quite common. I found it difficult to fathom whether she had genuine reason to be afraid or if this was just part of her disease. Her murder would suggest that she perhaps had a legitimate reason to be frightened. I feel guilty for not taking her anxiety seriously enough.'

'Was she afraid of someone in the family?'

'Now this is veering towards a proper police interrogation,' he says jokingly. 'Honestly, I could not identify exactly who or what she was afraid of. But I would not rule out someone in the family. Certainly not.'

She wants to be careful with him, not press too hard and risk losing his cooperation. Besides, she can decipher what he is trying to tell her through this code of half-revelations and his eagerness to speak to her after the funeral. Ahona's fear was not just an undefined anxiety but a more specific fear: She was afraid that someone in her family might do her harm.

She decides to draw him out instead. 'You are a psychiatrist. I was under the impression that you prescribe the medications while counsellors who don't have a medical degree do the talking and listening. I am sorry to be so crude but my knowledge of medicine is really limited.'

'You are not being crude. That's how it normally works. But I prefer to do both myself. I have always believed that it helps the process of therapy if the psychiatrist is also the counsellor. Besides, I have worked a lot in the smaller cities where there is a stigma attached to mental health problems. Hospitals have started offering psychiatric care but the departments are invariably a one-man army. I didn't always have the luxury of having a psychologist to help me. I have become used to doing both. Incidentally, Dr Sen also followed the same practice for some of his more difficult patients like Ahona.'

'Did you grow up in the South?' Sohini asks.

He looks surprised.

'I have an ear for accents,' Sohini says. 'You don't have a heavy southern accent but I can make out that you've lived there a good bit. I can also tell you that the inflections are from Tamil Nadu, not from Kerala or Andhra Pradesh. I spent a couple of years in Madras, I'm sorry, I should say Chennai, when I was in middle school. My father was transferred there.'

'I'm impressed. Henry Higgins in flesh and blood! I must have seen *My Fair Lady* at least ten times when I was a child. I have a friend who is a doctor in Edinburgh who can tell you which county you come from by your accent. But it's easier to tell the difference with English accents, isn't it? Coming back to your question, I went to school all over Tamil Nadu, although I was born here and lived here till I was nine. Then my parents moved to the South. My father was in a transferable job. I got my degrees from

Pondicherry – my MBBS in 1992, but it was a long slog before I finally got my postgraduate degree. I have been all over the South – Salem, Coimbatore, even did a short stint in Mangalore.'

'What brings you back to this city? When did you move here?'

'A couple of things. I was in a long relationship that ended recently. She was married and finally didn't get a divorce. I thought I would just get back to my roots, the healing touch of my home town. The Americans make such a fuss over it, don't they? So I told myself, why not give it a shot. Besides, I wanted to live in a city. I'm a little tired of the provinciality of small towns.'

'Do you have family or friends here?'

'Not really. My parents passed away almost a decade ago in Chennai. I have lost touch with my boyhood friends but I am sure I will find them at some club or party. I've just been very busy with work – haven't even rented a proper flat. I am staying in one of those service flats at Edwards Mansion on Bishop's Row. I have got to a point where I am beginning to get really sick of the place.'

As they leave, they pass the reception again. The receptionist looks intimidated and Sohini decides to be kind to her. 'Thank you,' she says. 'Your job must be difficult, handling all these patients and their relatives. They can be so unreasonable at times. What is your name?'

She looks a little startled and then in a nervous gesture

points to a small nameplate pinned to her sari and says, 'Chaitali…Chaitali Mitra.'

---

Arjun went through six months of counselling after the accident that took away his wife, son and father. He had found the exercise futile. He was always a reserved person, protective of his personal space, and his loss had made him withdraw even more. Thus his six-month-long attempt to unclutter his mind and heal his grief had largely comprised long questions from the therapist and monosyllabic answers from him. The very idea of revealing his deepest, most private thoughts to a complete stranger made him so visibly anxious and unsettled that the counsellor had herself suggested that they end their sessions.

He thinks their meeting with Sandip was as much a waste of time as his many hours sitting in his counsellor's stuffy clinic every Friday afternoon. If it was up to him, he would have insisted on getting more details of Ahona's interactions with Sandip, patient confidentiality be damned. This was a murder investigation after all. He feels frustrated and a little annoyed with Sohini for going so easy on the doctor.

After politely declining her offer of a lift he crosses the road, buys a loose cigarette and starts walking. It's about an hour's walk home. He needs that time to clear his head and organize his thoughts.

# 16

# The Sniper Sniped

Arjun notices that *Aaj Porjonto*'s increasingly high-pitched smear campaign has begun to affect the investigation. Sohini seems distracted at the interviews, clearly brooding over something all the time, and often loses her train of thought when she speaks to him, stopping mid-sentence with a baffled expression. It is also obvious that she has been drinking heavily in the mornings. He decides to tell her about Bulai Saha. Arjun seems squeamish about talking about this particular case at the police station. She suggests a coffee house near their office.

This cafe has clearly seen better times. The high ceiling, a pristine white a couple of decades ago, has acquired a permanent patina of dust and cigarette smoke. There are cobwebs so intricate and large that they seem like carefully crafted filigree work. The cafe's coffee and the thickly bread-crumbed fish fries that they still serve were the local office-goers' staple just a decade ago. It has not withstood the assault of the new cafe chains well, with their English-speaking baristas, their puffs, rolls and pastries, and smileys on the cappuccino foam.

The cafe now attracts stragglers – tired medical salesmen with their trademark briefcases and cheap polyester ties, penurious job-seekers who want a quiet moment to browse through recruitment forms and the occasional couple keeping an assignation. As they sip weak, tepid coffee Arjun speaks in a low voice, secure in the fact that the drone of the old-fashioned ceiling fans will thwart even the keenest eavesdropper.

---

Bulai Saha is a rotund man in his early forties. He rarely wears a shirt or vest and is usually found at his tea shop clad in a green lungi, his chest and paunch glistening with sweat as he listens to Bengali film songs that sound a little distorted and crackly on his cheap cellphone. There is a truck repair workshop across the road from his shop, the main source of his custom. For snacks he serves homemade biscuits, moori with aubergine and potato fritters that drip with mustard oil. On demand, he chops onion and green chillies with the moori. His wife, Deepmala, a small, dark woman, serves a basic meal of rice and fish curry for lunch that is popular with the drivers. This is occasionally followed by sandesh on the days that Bulai shops in the main market of the nearby town.

Bulai is proud of the small strip of land that he owns adjacent to the tea shop where he grows radish in winter, bitter gourd and bhindi in summer. There is a stunted kalojam tree right in the centre of his strip of land. He finds the fruit quite inedible and allows the neighbourhood children to pluck and eat the berries.

Of late, Bulai has been worried. Customers have noticed the frown lines slowly appearing on his face and the fidgety drumming of his fingers on the tea kettle. 'Is something the matter?' many of them have asked. 'You look as if you are headed to the gallows.'

The source of Bulai's anxiety is his piece of land. It is right on the rather narrow road that many refer to as the highway these days. It also happens to lie between Archishman Basu's massive farmhouse and the road. The consequence is that access to the farmhouse is pitifully narrow and big vehicles have to engage in complex manoeuvres to enter the property. Archishman offers to buy his land at a slight premium to the market rate but Bulai makes it clear that he is not interested in selling.

'Please understand, babu,' with folded hands he tells Archishman's secretary, Sunil Roy, who makes the offer, 'I am not asking for more money. This bit of land has been with us for three generations. I have deep ties to this little strip of land.'

When money fails to do the trick, threats follow. A group of young men accost him on his way home in the evening and ask him to part with his plot but this time the offer is reduced considerably. He tries to reason with them and since some of the faces are familiar he is not too intimidated. However, these encounters continue and the threats become more aggressive.

'You will leave a widow behind soon,' one of them says. 'She will make tea for the truckers while your ghost haunts the blackberry tree.'

Bulai finally takes the threats to heart. He says he will reconsider his decision and plans to take the matter to the village panchayat.

Two days after this encounter his body is found lying on the edge of a marsh less than a kilometre away from the village. He is found lying face up with an inexplicably serene expression; the previous night's rain has washed away the blood from the deep gash on his forehead. The rain has come down in a gentle patter from a tropical depression formed in the bay a few hundred kilometres away. The smell of the wet earth has masked the stench of decay. All this has given Bulai dignity in his untimely death. Even the jackals known to prey on the corpses of dead animals have stayed away.

Deepmala tells the panchayat about the threats. The entire village is incensed and lays siege to the local police station. Some of the protesters are carrying scythes and bamboo sticks and, roused from his afternoon siesta, the junior officer who heads the station fires his ancient Smith and Wesson revolver in the air.

The case has a clear link to the city via Archishman and thus the city's crime branch is involved. Arjun is assigned the case and, with Constable Sushanto Boral, climbs on a local train headed for the town that borders Bulai's village. The train, like all 'locals', as they are referred to, halts at every station, however small, and when Arjun and Sushanto finally reach, they are drenched in sweat and feel as though they have been gassed by the body odour of the hundreds of fellow commuters with whom they have shared their peanut-shell-littered compartment.

This is a policeman's dream case, rich in motive and evidence. Deepmala has identified three of the group that threatened Bulai. Arjun has also had a curious stroke of luck. He has received a message with an attached video clip from an unknown number. The clip has been recorded clandestinely on a cellphone. It is jerky and its resolution poor.

Despite these problems of quality, Archishman Basu can be seen clearly. He is seated on a sofa with a white slip cover. There is another man seated next to him, his face is unfamiliar and the thick gold chain around his neck glints as it catches the bright light shining from a lamp above. He is visibly agitated and is shouting at a group of men whose backs can be seen. 'I asked you to threaten him, you bastards, not to kill him. Whose idea was it to murder the runt?' he asks. While the men stand in penitent silence, Archishman speaks. 'If I get into trouble with the police, I'll make sure you all hang, you sisterfuckers.'

Arjun traces the video message to none other than Sunil Roy. Enquiries reveal that Sunil Roy had been fired a month ago for embezzlement from the petty cash chest but Archishman had insisted that he serve a notice period and come in every day to sort out his papers under the supervision of the company's chief accountant and a burly security guard. For this enforced diligence, Archishman has promised Roy not to file a complaint with the police. The clandestine recording and the fact that it is in Arjun's possession now is Sunil Roy's act of revenge.

However, as is common and one daresay acceptable in these niggling matters of crime committed by a crusading media baron as powerful as Archishman Basu, the investigation by the crime branch is suspended and the case transferred back to the local station. Arjun is a loyal foot soldier. His job is not to question or resist and he goes through the ritual of transferring his files without delay. But he keeps the video clip and makes sure it is saved on a number of pen drives that he hides carefully.

It is difficult even for the lowliest sepoy to entirely curb his curiosity about the fate of the case he had come so close to solving. On a Sunday afternoon two months later, Arjun finds himself at the police station where Bulai's corpse was brought by an irate crowd. The head constable in charge that afternoon is friendly and shows him the FIR of the murder. Arjun is hardly surprised that it bears no resemblance to the one he had so carefully read when he started his investigation. Two arrests have been made but he does not recognize the names.

He is also not shocked one bit when he is informed that Deepmala now lives in a small flat in one of the better neighbourhoods of the district town. Tongues have wagged but Deepmala has insisted that the capital for the flat has come from the sale of her land to the kind Mr Basu. If one goes by the stray quotes on the price of flats in her neighbourhood, Deepmala would have been paid roughly four times what Bulai had first been offered.

---

As Sohini and Arjun walk towards Basu's office on the fringes of the district, they pass Sunil Roy's cabin. The offices are in an old heritage building that has been refurbished extensively and includes among other things a large LED television screen outside that beams Basu's channel for roughly twelve hours during the day. The cabins inside all have glass fronts and Sunil Roy, as the head of circulation, has been given a singularly large one. The video might not have put Archishman Basu behind bars as the pilferer of petty cash would then have wished but it has ensured him a rather meteoric rise in professional status. As he sees them

Roy seems surprised but there is also a fleeting flicker of fear that crosses his face.

Archishman had initially refused to meet them. But Arjun had persisted and when he hinted they wanted to strike a 'deal' the media baron had relented. His office is surprisingly cramped with two computer consoles, stacks of files with old newspaper clippings and two large television sets.

He sounds unexpectedly apologetic when he meets them, eager to explain to Sohini that he bears her no ill will but it is the imperatives of competition in his industry that have driven his campaign. Arjun interrupts him by quietly putting his mobile phone on his table and switching the video clip on.

Archishman does a quick calculation. If he drops this exposé abruptly, his advertising revenues will plummet and hc will face a number of uncomfortable questions from his detractors. He thinks of the cost. Apart from his readers and viewers who are fiercely loyal to him, he is not a popular man. This video clip, the size of a few hundred bytes on a tiny storage device, has the power of a short but high Richter earthquake. It could, if it got into the wrong hands and indeed he can in a moment think of many such hands, lead to the collapse of his carefully built personal life and his empire.

'This campaign stops now,' he says with a flourish he refuses to abandon. 'We will also slip in some kind of apology saying that our sources misled us. Would you like some coffee?'

When they get into Sohini's car she gently touches Arjun's upper arm. There are many emotions playing in her mind, gratitude, the need to apologize for her inability to appreciate his contribution to the investigation, but all she can muster is a terse 'Thank you'.

She sees Arjun flinch at her touch; he murmurs something like 'It is my duty, madam' and stares straight ahead as if to ward off further display of intimacy.

# 17

# Closure

It's been eight days since the murder. There have been no arrests, not even a communiqué from the police confirming that they have suspects. The city's middle class is growing vocal about the police force's ineptitude, egged on by an increasingly strident press. Murders are a dime a dozen in this state and usually find a small mention on the inside pages of the dailies. However, Ahona's is a special murder, a high-society murder in a high-society neighbourhood.

Ahona's former classmates organize a candlelight vigil at her college, which two of the institution's more distinguished alumni, an actress and a bestselling Bengali author, attend. The sombre silence at the vigil captures some of the anxiety that hangs like a pall over the city that, left unaddressed, could affect the results of three key by-elections due in three weeks. There have been calls for a probe by a central agency, based in faraway Delhi, led by Tarok Panda, the scourge of the treasury benches in the state assembly. He insists that a political motive for the murder should be explored.

Probir Banerjee, the city's harried police commissioner, summons Sohini and Arjun to his office located right next to the crime branch. Banerjee has been a peripatetic cop with secondments in Delhi, with the Interpol in Bangkok and a sabbatical at Harvard's Kennedy School of Government, where he has acquired a degree in public administration. He is known to be malleable, eager to do his political masters' bidding but otherwise honest and a straight-talker. He is also a numbers cop, fixated on the city's crime statistics and the rate of what he likes to call 'closure'.

The meeting between him and the two detectives is brief and they barely get a chance to sit before Banerjee gives his instructions and concludes the meeting. 'We need an arrest by tomorrow. There has to be some perception of closure on the case,' he says.

Sohini and Arjun have been prepared for this. These demands for impressions of progress, of token arrests when even the barest of chargesheets are ready, are common. However, 'closure' in the correct sense of the word can come only from a confession that is signed and sealed before a magistrate under Section 164 of the Indian Penal Code. Neither of them believes that this will be easy. Their tack is to identify a couple of suspects, get judicial custody and leak little bits of information to the press that is part truth, part fabrication. They hope it will keep the press at bay for a while. If they are very lucky, they will get their killer. They have two suspects in mind – Saikat and Raju, Shonjoy's temporary driver who had threatened Ahona.

Their case against Raju is simple. He had threatened Ahona and claimed to possess a weapon similar to the one that DCM claims was used for the beheading. However, both detectives wonder if an ill-educated young migrant would be able to execute such a sophisticated murder. Nevertheless, the city has a history of unlettered killers who have covered their tracks with copybook meticulousness. Thus Raju is as much of a suspect as the young, mendacious mathematician.

---

The gloves have come off in handling Saikat. Three constables from the uniformed division accost him at his institute, bundle him into a police van and bring him to the police station. The questioning takes place in one of the officially designated interrogation rooms. Some thought appears to have gone into its decor, clearly designed to unsettle the suspect or, as the interrogators hope, instil a sense of fear. The assumption, of course, is that fear elicits the truth. An assumption that has been questioned by many criminologists.

The room has a single wooden table illuminated by a

bare bulb. The bulb is high wattage and hangs low on the suspect's side so that it disorients the suspect and then induces a dull but nagging headache. The chair for the suspect is straight-backed and without armrests. The other side of the table has two somewhat more comfortable chairs for the questioners. The windows are shut and the panes covered with what seems like black chart paper. The overall effect is of a chiaroscuro.

As he walks into the room where Sohini and Arjun wait ready with their case file and tape recorder, Saikat seems unfazed by the prospect of interrogation. In fact, the detectives are surprised to notice the trace of a smirk on his face.

'You have lied to us, Saikat,' Sohini begins quietly.

Saikat's smirk becomes more pronounced and, before she can continue, he interrupts her. 'So you've heard the unofficial version of my exploits in the US. I'm sorry I told you the official story but it's the one that everyone here knows. You can hardly blame me for sticking to it in my first interaction with you.'

Sohini continues in her quiet voice but there is a subtle change in tone. 'That's not the only lie. You could not have been at the computer centre, as you claimed, on the evening of the murder. The centre was closed. If you think you can get away with all this because your uncle is supposedly an influential man, you are wrong.'

The rest of what she says startles both Arjun and Saikat.

Her voice does not quaver but her flat monotone carries an abrupt, unexpected ferocity. She has always found this an effective technique – the sudden invocation of menace; the quiet threat of violence has more power to unsettle than the act of violence itself.

'You might think I am an idiot. But if you continue lying, this idiotic woman who is asking you these stupid questions will string you from the ceiling and beat you up so badly that your bastard uncle Chanchal will find it difficult to even recognize you. You thought you were violent with that poor Korean student. Let me show you what violence is.'

The smugness and smirk have gone. Saikat is shaking like a leaf and the grimace on his face tells the detectives that he is desperately trying to fight back impending sobs. He had expected an outburst from Sohini that he hoped to counter with his bravado. But the tone in which she has threatened him, a tone that one would use to discuss the weather or offer a cup of tea, has terrified him with the sheer credibility it carries. It tells him this frail woman, with the dark half-moons under her eyes, is capable of carrying out her threat.

The sobs finally come and he tells them, 'I was at Urmi's room that evening and night. We are in a relationship. She is an MSc student and I teach one of her courses. The faculty – even junior faculty members like me – are expressly forbidden to have anything to do with students beyond the classroom and office hours. If anyone gets to know about our affair and that we spent that night together, both of us will be dismissed from the institute. It would be very difficult for either of us to find somewhere else to go to. Ratna, Urmi's friend, was with us till around ten in the evening and you can ask her if you think Urmi will lie to save my skin. I swear I am not lying and I beseech you to keep this to yourself.'

Sohini remains calm. 'We will check with them but god help you if you are lying. However, we are not the moral police. How you choose to spend your evenings is your business and you can rest assured that we have better things to do than tattle to your colleagues.'

Both detectives know that for once Saikat is not lying. They will have to bet on Raju now.

---

Raju's slum is for the poorest of the poor – the unwanted migrant, the glue-sniffing adolescent ragpicker, the hookers who spread their legs for less than the price of a packet of chips, the recently castrated eunuch nursing her infection – this is their sanctuary. The city gives up its sovereignty on its edges and abdicates all its civic responsibilities there. Wide sewers flow Styx-like along the sides of the narrow entrance and there are flotillas of turds and dead rats visible on the viscous surface. There are packs of mangy dogs. They look feral but the residents know that the pigs, their underbellies and legs coated with the muck of the sewers, are the ones to really fear.

One hand-operated tube well can be seen, which presumably supplies the water for all the households. The stench from a row of communal toilets combines with the smell of burning garbage to create a miasma that hangs all over. The shanties that flank the lane are made of a mix of brick, tin, asbestos and different kinds of waterproofing material scoured from the city's dumps.

Shonjoy's temp job was Raju's last driving job. He now works as a henchman for Khonda Babloo, the slumlord. He is a regular at the hooch shop that is like any of the other shanties except that it has a cart selling boiled eggs and roasted peanuts right outside.

He hasn't been difficult to trace. The city cannot afford a mesh of closed circuit television cameras or the sophisticated gadgetry that modern eavesdropping depends on. On the other hand, the police have a large and reliable network of informants. They take particular care to keep tabs on migrants, especially after terror attacks in other cities. A slightly demented petty thug with a driver's licence hasn't posed much of a challenge to this human radar.

When they arrest him, he is rolling drunk and itching for a brawl. There is a feistiness in him that the three constables try their best to subdue but it lingers even when he is sitting in the same interrogation room that Saikat had recently occupied with its shadeless lamp and straight-backed, armless chair.

# 18

# Raju

A surprisingly large number of young men from the working class like to adopt the nickname Raju though it might not share a single syllable with the name their parents chose for them. It gets them acceptance, or so they believe, in a contemporary milieu, a much desired city-slickness and freedom from their double-barrelled and archaic birth-names with their invariable references to gods and goddesses.

Shonjoy's temporary driver was born Shiv Pujan Mahto in a small village just about fifty kilometres east of the main town of a district that borders Bihar and Uttar Pradesh. The map shows the village as a part of Uttar Pradesh. The adjacency blurs identities and many in the district, including Shiv Pujan's family, think of themselves as Biharis.

Shiv Pujan was sixteen when the drought started. Poor cognitive abilities made him drop out of school in sixth grade but he discovered other talents. His two sisters were married when they were fifteen and one of the fathers-in-law had an ancient Ambassador that he used as a taxi. The car ferried passengers from this cluster of villages to the weekly cattle market, the district town and the small railway station where a few passenger trains stop. The learning disabilities, to everyone's surprise, did not affect Shiv Pujan's ability to learn to drive this beast of a car and he chipped in as a part-time driver for this automobile ferry.

He also started to frequent the local brewery. He drank to get drunk and his drunkenness often led to fierce brawls with the regulars at the drinking hole. His pugnaciousness attracted the attention of a local landlord who gave him freelance work of collecting rent and occasionally evicting defaulters. For work of this kind, he believed a personal weapon was essential. He had heard of Rampuri knives with their lethal blades of steel and wanted one. However, a government ban on many of the variants meant that they were in short supply. What he got instead was a small cleaver with a wooden handle and a blade that needed to be sharpened regularly. He swaddled it in layers of cloth like a baby and hid it carefully at the bottom of a gym bag bought at the village fair. The bag had three misspelt logos – Adidas, Nike and Reebok – imprinted on its side.

The drought persisted into the next sowing season and the demand for hired hands dwindled further. The Mahto family had heard of the new government programme that guaranteed work for a hundred days in the year but its munificence had not reached their part of the state yet. His father forced him to join a small band of workers that included himself, his older son and some neighbours to board a train that took them to the state's capital. There they embarked on a seemingly endless train journey to the North.

—

The first thing that strikes Shiv Pujan when he arrives at their destination two days later is that it is a rich state, far richer than his own. The fields are larger, with tractors and mechanical threshers everywhere. Even the village roads are well paved and the canals are full to the brim with water fetched from a large dam. There are power-operated sprinklers that fascinate him.

His dislike for his temporary home grows quickly. He is used to the summer heat that bakes his village for a good four months of the year but that is no match for the cruel, arid hotness of this place that does not dissipate even in the darkest hour of the night. Their room with a corrugated tin roof is like an oven and when he pisses in the morning he notices that the stream is brown.

When he gets his first day off after a week of work, he explores the nearby town. He leaves the main street with the post office and bus station. As he wanders into the small lanes that branch off, he realizes that this is drug country. There are signs of it everywhere – the squatting men huddling together for a communal puff of ganja or smack, the used rusty heroin needles littered everywhere and the abundance of silver foil from cigarette packets with their telltale holes in the middle. On his second visit to the town he finds himself sharing a charpai with a group of smackheads. He has introduced himself as Raju. The name stays with him though his family and close friends continue to call him Shibu.

When they return home that autumn after the harvest Raju looks visibly older. It is difficult to tell whether it is the harsh northern sun or the dope that he is addicted to that has turned his skin so leathery and lined his face. His father had noticed his son's drugged eyes in the hot evenings but dismissed it as a phase in his son's life that would pass once they returned to the clemency of their own climes.

But it does not. Raju is an addict and no amount of the local hooch can get him the high that he has experienced. He has to make do with the ganja and the occasional supply of charas available in the village but his body craves a chemical hit.

The regular use of narcotics has induced a distinct shift in his personality. The constant anger and the compulsive need to brawl give way to a sullen moodiness punctuated by a violence that is more visceral, more brutal than earlier.

The following October, the family decide to try their luck in the North again. Raju's ability to work has suffered, he has fallen out with his father, but he insists on going with the gang from the village. His body craves a stronger drug and he fantasizes about a rubber pipe tied tightly on his arm and a needle shooting up heroin into his veins.

If the summer months were unbearable, the winter is worse. What he hates most is the damp fog that seems to seep in through the nostrils and find its way into both his brain and lungs. He has a hacking cough through their first fortnight that rattles his bones and leaves him with a weary, aching body.

On a chilly but mercifully clear morning in mid January Raju runs away with his small bag and a couple of thousand rupees stolen from the workers' common fund kept aside for emergencies. A tractor taxi drops him at the railway station, where he takes a train to Delhi. He wants to get as far away from the cold and fog as possible and decides on the large city in the East that he has heard of so much from his cousins but has never had a chance to visit. The journey takes him two days in a general compartment.

Raju has spent a year in this city. His days of unemployment and homelessness are short. The network of migrants from Bihar and eastern Uttar Pradesh is close-knit and resourceful. He is offered a job by a taxi driver from his district who rents his cab from his malik for a night shift. He becomes a cleaner, a factotum who sits to the driver's left essentially to handle the odd drunk passenger who either gets violent or gets into a loud row over the inflated fare that they charge. He also takes the wheel when the driver is too sleepy or drunk. The routine suits him. He gets his fix of smack in the morning, sleeps through the day, has a bath in the evening at the hand-operated tube well and turns up punctually at nine for his shift.

Within six months he is confident enough about the city's maze of roads to offer his services as a 'badli' or temp, filling in when regular drivers are away. He continues to live in a slum near the dockyards – a narrow space in a small room that sleeps six, keeping his clothes and cleaver in a small bag stowed behind his pillow like a bed's headboard. In November, approximately ten months before Ahona's murder, Shankar Mahto, a roommate and a badli, tells him that a Chatterjee saheb who lives in the midtown area is looking for a driver for a few weeks.

—

He knows this evening will turn out badly as soon as she gets into the car. She is dressed in black and her long sleeves accentuate her bony gauntness. She does not reciprocate his 'namaste' and as soon as he changes gears and picks up speed, she admonishes him with a curt 'Slow down. Drive carefully.' He drops her off at the Goethe Institut for her concert and, as he opens the door for her, she instructs him to wait for her at the gate at nine sharp and not a second later. Instead of parking, he drives south where he knows of a country liquor bar. He plans to have half a pint of the XXX Special to relax, take the edge off the day and forget the haughty girl's rudeness. At the bar with its grimy polyester curtain and the low wooden benches, he finds three of his cabbie friends.

They are drinking and passing around a joint that they claim is charas. By the time he has finished a pint and the ten-odd tokes of the two spliffs that have been passed around he thinks he is dying. There are voices in his head and they are not just talking to him but taking a hammer to his skull. He passes out and when he wakes up it is eleven at night. They carry him to the car and one of his friends drives him back to Shonjoy's house. Raju does not remember the address and he can barely speak but has one of Shonjoy's business cards in his pocket that he hands over. He is sprawled on the back seat when he arrives at Shonjoy's flat. The guards create a ruckus but they ignore them. The car is parked in the basement and despite the guards' resistance he spends the night in the car.

Next morning when he faces Shonjoy, he knows that his already brief tenure as his badli is over. Shonjoy is screaming at him but his ordeal does not end there. He will get his dues only after he goes and apologizes to Ahona. He rings her bell, head bowed in penitence, hands folded in a gesture of supplication. She opens the door and starts shouting at him. He can take the shouting, all that venom, the 'You lazy, irresponsible bastards you should be sent back to the boondocks you came from', but when she raises her hand as if to strike, the voices in his head suddenly start screaming. He grips her wrist and tells her, 'I will kill you, you witch. Like all the other heads I chopped off with my cleaver. I can show it to you. It's in my bag right here.'

---

Sohini sits back as Arjun interrogates Raju. These are accusations rather than questions and Arjun keeps repeating them like a mantra. This repetitive insinuation delivered with its own distinct cadence has worked in the past. Arjun hopes that there will be a point when this rhythmic incantation will break the suspect and bring the truth out.

'Tell me why you killed her. Did you chop her head off because she shouted at you? Did you do it to prove your manhood, to get your dick up, you swine? Did the sight of her blood turn you on? Did you wash the cleaver in the bathroom?'

Raju has brought his feet up on the chair trying to assume a fetal position, hugging his knees and burying his head between them. This is precarious – not only is the chair too small for him but he is trying to rock back and forth. He is muttering to himself and it sounds like a litany that is difficult to comprehend. Arjun can barely make out the words '*Nahi mara*' (Did not kill).

Sohini asks him to take a break. Raju's nicotine-stained

fingers tell Arjun that he is a heavy smoker. He fishes out his own packet and slides it across the table along with a lighter. Raju stops rocking and pulls out a cigarette from the pack and then flicks the lighter. He does both with his left hand. Arjun wants to make sure. He asks the guard outside to fetch a piece of paper and he pulls out his cheap jotter and hands it to Raju. 'Write your name now,' he commands.

Both Raju and Sohini look bewildered. Raju tentatively reaches for the pen.

'Now, now!' Arjun shouts.

Raju alias Shiv Pujan Mahto scrawls his name on the piece of paper with his left hand. Arjun and Sohini both realize that Raju is left-handed. If the city police's top forensic expert's opinion is correct, as it usually is, the killer is right-handed; Raju could not be the killer. Any competent lawyer who looks at the evidence sheet and Durga Maity's assessment note neatly clipped on to it would kill the case in a courtroom in a matter of seconds. However, the chance of someone like Raju Mahto, a petty thug from one of the darkest, dankest slums of the city, hiring a half-competent counsel is remote. The detectives decide to ask for an extension of his custody. He thus becomes the twelfth man, the bench-warmer, the stand-in, the Plan B who is to be called in to play if all else fails. The police press officer makes an announcement that they have finally made progress.

# 19

# An Affair

Late September nights can get quite cold in Shimla. The family is here on vacation escaping the muggy heat that the end of monsoons brings to their city along with the mosquitoes and the outbreak of malaria and jaundice. Durga Puja is early this year and schools and colleges are shut for three weeks. Ever since she was a child, she hated the carnival frenzy that the festival brings to the city. All she associates with it is the swell of crowds, many of them from faraway villages, their unwashed smell and the maddening traffic, honking horns adding to the cacophony of multiple loudspeakers.

Despite her protestations – she is twelve, on the brink of adolescence, and demands her own room – she has been asked to share a room with him. Mercifully the room has twin beds, the least she could expect. It is ten at night and she has tucked herself into the bed under the thick quilt with its cotton slip-cover and comforting smell of fresh laundry. She is exhausted from the frantic driving the whole day – morning in Mashobra, picnic lunch in the fir forests of Naldehra and the rush back into town to hear the army band play in the small church. But she is not sleepy yet.

Mountain roads make her edgy with all their twists and turns and the fear of a careless driver hurtling towards them invisibly from the other side of a hairpin bend. She can still feel the adrenaline coursing through her veins. He has switched off the light but she hears him tossing and turning. After about fifteen minutes, she hears him rise, slip on a sweater and pad across to her bed. He lifts her duvet and slips in beside her and gently puts his arm around her. After her initial shock at this unexpected transgression, she realizes that she no longer feels the urge to repel. She reciprocates and puts her arm around him. All this happens in complete silence. There is nothing more comforting than the warmth of a body next to you on a cold mountain night. They hold each other and fall asleep.

They follow the predictable trajectory of an affair in bloom, going beyond the prissiness of adolescent romance into a more adult, carnal domain. There are the usual milestones of the progress of their intimacy. The swell of a breast and the hardness of the phallus felt through layers of clothing is followed within weeks by the lying bare. Recalcitrant hooks, clasps and zippers present their delightful challenges.

She is, however, apprehensive about the next step, the 'going all the way', that quaint phrase that she has heard more sexually tutored school friends use to describe the finality of consummation.

Despite her fears and misgivings this too happens on a humid June afternoon in an apartment temporarily empty. He produces a condom, one of those imported ones brought from a roadside vendor that claims to be flavoured with chocolate, a couple of towels are spread on the bed and she bends her knees and splays her legs. It is quick, disappointingly so for her with just a jab of pain, a muffled cry, a few drops of blood on the towels and a soreness that goes away in minutes.

They marvel at the power that they have over each other's bodies, of the complex play of hormones that creates this need to feed off each other's bodies. At first they are careful. They take care to fuck only if there is no one around and always protected by the thin wall of latex.

But then they begin to test their luck. The fact that she is not a screamer or moaner helps. He learns to keep a supply of condoms hidden at accessible locations.

However, as the frequency of their trysts increases they become more reckless. There is a party one evening. They say their usual 'hellos' to the guests and retire to his room. It gets raucous outside. Someone has brought a guitar and is playing Elvis Presley songs. They can hear the thud of feet as couples start dancing. He does not have a condom today and she is afraid. He explains that he will pull out at the right time, that coitus interruptus is known to work in most cases. The singer breaks into a shouty 'Hound Dog' with three basic chords. The thrum of the dancing reaches a peak. He pulls out but has a niggling fear that he is too late.

She misses her period and breaks into a panic. Her classes at school are a blur as the fear gnaws at her relentlessly. His efforts at solace are empty. She decides to tell her father.

# 20

# Intimacy

These fits of rage descend on Arjun suddenly and without notice. It is a rage against the unfairness of the road accident that took away his wife, son and father in a matter of minutes if not seconds, a blinding anger towards the bastard truck driver who failed to press his brake in time, who tried to flee after he had killed them, terrified by the fear of mob lynching. But there is also an anger that he harbours towards himself, towards the selfishness of his grief. His constant hysterical refrain as they sedated him at the hospital after he saw their bodies was *'Amar ki hobe?'* (What will happen to me?)

The rage that boils over today, he suspects, has been triggered by his verbal assault on Raju. He turns violent as usual in the privacy of his bedroom, breaks things, punches the wall until his knuckles bleed. He stops only when sheer physical exhaustion calms him down and he can hear his mother's anxious voice, 'Aru, open the door. Open it please…'

He unlocks the door, steps outside and sees his mother. They have never been physically demonstrative, afraid to touch or hug. But in this frail old woman's eyes he sees a steely resolve to protect her son from the dangers that might come his way, from the demons that he cannot banish from his mind.

She says, 'Wash your hands. Put Dettol on your cuts. If any of them are deep, put a Band-Aid. Dinner's ready. I was waiting for you.'

'Give me a minute,' he says.

This is what he likes about his mother – the lack of fuss, curiosity or judgement. She accepts him as he is, with all his kinks and flaws, but he is aware of her deep, unexpressed empathy. This exchange of two simple sentences is their moment of intimacy.

---

She finds herself drawn to this man in their very first encounter. She has always been needy, eager to seek recompense for what her parents with their whirlwind lives have failed to give her. What appeals to her most is that his attention does not seem to stray from her even for a moment.

She had hardly expected to open up to another person so easily, to tell him about her innermost and darkest fears.

The fear of being judged, labelled and then shunned has always held her back. She surprises herself when she finds herself talking almost in a gush about her adolescence, the relationship that scarred her both emotionally and physically that she still finds so difficult to jettison. She went to a Catholic missionary school and she is familiar with the idea of confession. She thinks of this man as a priest endowed with the power to forgive her sins. She wants so desperately to atone, to be forgiven.

---

The news of Raju's incarceration makes it to the front pages of all the city's dailies. Arjun finds one headline in a Bangla paper particularly amusing. The press and television announcement about Raju is made by DC Dipayan Mukherjee and the headline simply says 'DC Let-You-Know Lets Us Know'. It is not a clever play of words, not a complex double entendre and is certainly not one of the best of the city's wordsmiths' oeuvre. It has, however, a simple straightforward punch that appeals to him and he starts laughing. As Sohini enters the office he shows it to her. He is still laughing and the laughter is infectious. Sohini joins in and they find themselves suddenly sharing their first moment of light-hearted camaraderie.

These are the small intimacies of the workplace that bring colleagues together. It creates a bond, a certain mutual understanding and trust, that often remains confined to the domain of work.

Sohini was touched by Arjun's effort to shield her from *Aaj Porjonto*'s brutal attack but she is uncomfortable that she owes him one, that he might demand a quid pro quo later. She senses that Arjun seems to expect nothing in return but she remains guarded.

Still, they trust each other a little more than when they started on the case, on that rainy evening after Ahona's murder. Their visits to the derelict coffee shop where they first discussed Bulai Saha grow more frequent. But their conversation remains confined to their work and their cases. Arjun refers to his 'favourite' case, childlike, as if he was referring to a toy. This turns out to be the infamous university degree forgery case that had hogged the headlines a few years ago.

Sohini prefers to talk about her experience at the civil defence department. As she tells him the story, she begins to discover in retrospect the funnier side of her years spent there. Both of them laugh as she tells him about the murderous politicking that went on over the location of the new water cooler, her assistant Mullick's nifty pilfering of fried fish from the office canteen, the pompous officiousness of some of the home guards and Ram Bahadur's persistent demand for a khaki beret that he thought would impress his neighbours.

Although they do not discuss their personal lives there are similarities that perhaps subliminally strengthen their bond. Neither of them has families in the conventional sense of the word nor partners. Both have to care for an ageing parent. But most important, Sohini and Arjun are both of an age when they crave a sudden spark of energy to renew their lives but find it elusive, find that it is all too late to start all over again.

—

After many months, Shonjoy and Atreyi find themselves sitting next to each other on the sofa. He holds his face in his hands and sobs gently. Despite the bitterness, the anger and her disappointment, she reaches out and tries to touch his face through the shield of his palms. It is a spontaneous gesture of empathy for a man she once loved, an involuntary concession towards his bereavement. He flinches first but then bends towards her as if he wants to be cradled, to let her share in his loss.

However, she resists and suddenly the venom, the black bile that has accumulated in her, the hatred for this man are back. She says, 'Shonjoy, I need to talk to you.'

He hopes what she says will bring a reconciliation, build a bridge across the chasm that has divided them over these years. 'Tell me,' he says entreatingly.

She says his name again in a show of assertion and firmness and then he realizes that their divide will widen much further.

'Shonjoy, I want a divorce,' Atreyi says.

# 21

# Shoriker Dhal

**Thirty-five years ago**

The sleepy hamlet called Shoriker Dhal does not have a proper railway platform, although the local trains make a minute-long stop there. Instead there is a rectangular patch of red earth that identifies itself as the place to alight in front of the shed that passes for the station. There are signboards on either side, the signage in regulation railway black on yellow bearing the name of this middle-of-nowhere train stop in both English and Bangla. The best way to get off a train is to simply jump off the stationary train with as much deftness as you can muster, leaving your luggage at the edge of the compartment door and quickly hauling it down once your feet are on the ground. It works well for the young and agile but for the others it presents an athletic challenge that occasionally leads to sprained, if not broken, ankles.

Shoriker Dhal is, however, not just one more of the many villages that dot the district, their existence recognized only by the meticulous surveyor drawing a map for land records. It has attained a certain degree of fame for the Kali temple that lies a couple of kilometres to the north.

The temple is the only surviving structure in the sprawling ruin that was once the mansion of the Roy Barman family, the zamindars who owned half the district until the forties. They were originally from Tripura, their origins visible in the slanted eyes and high cheekbones in the few surviving portraits of the Barman rajas that hang on the wall of the snake- and bat-infested *shodor ghor*, the hall. They were devout shaktas and the Kali idol that is still worshipped is rumoured to be at least three hundred years old.

Local history in this part of the world is often a blur of myths, disjointed facts and hearsay. Thus the reasons for the demise of this once powerful family or indeed how the worship of their family deity carried on after they were gone remain a mystery. However, the power of the goddess – to heal the most debilitating disease, to summon an armada of nimbus clouds that shower rain during the sowing season, to bring life into a long-barren womb – is the stuff of legend. The temple has a full-time priest and the throng of devotees peaks every fortnight on new moon nights when there is a special puja.

They have a farmhouse here that his grandfather built on the banks of the small river that flows past the cluster of villages. It is the only concrete structure there and it even has an electricity connection. The supply, though, is sparse and the principal source of light is the hot white glow of the hurricane lamps fuelled by kerosene that the caretaker, Keshto, lights at dusk.

Their visit to this farmhouse has become a ritual. They come here every year in early winter a few weeks after Kali Puja for an extended weekend. He has always looked forward to these visits, more because it means missing classes for a few days with his father's approval than a love for the countryside. Earlier they came as a family – his parents, grandfather, often some of his parents' friends, with their green hold-alls, black steel trunks and suitcases. Things have changed since then. He comes alone and Shonukaka, his father's distant cousin, chaperones him.

Poltu, Keshto's son, is about his age, always eager to please and also to impress. There is invariably a boyish cruelty about Poltu's exploits – the strangely hued lizard he has captured and decapitates; the non-venomous grass snakes that he winds around his arm and then mercilessly kills by holding them by the tail and thrashing them on the ground; the hive of wasps that he sets fire to with the kerosene-soaked rag tied to the end of a pole, both of them running for cover as the wasps disperse in an angry swarm; the calf he trips by kicking its hind legs back.

This is the first time they have come during Kali Puja. Shoriker Dhal is thrumming with the hordes of worshippers from all over the district – the dhakis beating their drums with a slow roll that escalates to an ecstatic crescendo, the bauls and fokirs doing their own gigs in the akhadas they have set up, the freak-show tents, the food vendors who are frying their delicacies so deep that there is a constant sizzle of oil that fills the air, the balloon sellers, the ice lolly men with their white Thermocol boxes.

The main puja is later that night, a new moon night. Poltu asks him, 'Do you want to see something really scary? I bet you'll shit in your pants when you see it.'

'I don't scare easily,' he replies.

'Let's have a wager.' Poltu pushes him hard. 'If you can see what I want to show you without feeling frightened, you can have my box of pebbles with the white patterns that you keep touching, and also the green grass snake in that jar. If you lose, you have to give me your HMT watch.'

He agrees and Poltu warns him, 'If Shonukaka or my father asks where we are going this evening, tell them that we are going to the baul akhada to listen to Aboni Baul.'

---

It's a long walk to the temple and by the time they reach it's almost nine. The temple courtyard is full of devotees, the dhakis are warming up and there seem to be hundreds of hurricane lamps lighting up the entire space with a hot white glow. A choking haze of incense and burnt sal bark fills the air. A group of boys in the corner have lit a long string of crackers that keep going off one after another like a machine gun.

There is a U-shaped wooden contraption in the middle, washed clean and dripping – the *haadikath*.

'What's that for?' he asks Poltu.

Poltu refuses to explain. 'Just wait a bit and you will find out,' he says.

He notices a small cluster of goats tethered to a pole in the corner. They seem restless and frightened by the crowds, lights and noise.

A group of men, all bare-bodied and wearing lungis, enter the courtyard. The drumbeats slowly build up and now someone starts beating on a small metallic gong. It is out of rhythm with the drums; its tinny harshness assails the ear and asserts its existence.

One of the men approaches the goats. They are trembling now, shitting copiously, and he can see the small turds dropping out of their rectums in a steady continuum that reminds him of a machine. It is as if some primeval, hardwired alarm has gone off in their tiny brains warning of danger ahead.

The man untethers one of the goats and he notices that there is another collar-like rope around its neck that the man uses to drag it towards the centre of the arena. There is a palpable increase in the excitement of the crowd. He notices that one of the men has a long cleaver with him. The goat is resisting, pulling back, still shitting, its hind legs shaking like a leaf.

The goat's neck is placed on the haadikath. A man crouches in front of the contraption and holds the goat's head steady. Three men hold the goat's legs from behind. The drumbeats rise to a crescendo and a man crouching on the side lifts his cleaver. He notices Poltu stealing a glance at him hoping he will win the wager.

There is a sudden acceleration in the swing of the cleaver as it makes its way to the goat's neck but he sees it in slow motion. His eyes dart between the arc of the cleaver and the terror in the goat's eyes. A fantasy enters his mind in the split of a nanosecond. He imagines himself holding the cleaver and bringing it down. However, instead of the goat it's his mother's head that he imagines in the wooden trap. Her hair has fallen to the side leaving her neck bare and he can see the two stray, errant strands of silver in the sea of lush black. The face of the man holding her head steady is blurred but the man who holds her legs down is Runumama, her distant cousin who visited her secretly in the afternoons when his father was away at work and the rest of the household deep in their afternoon siesta.

He can see the fear in his mother's eyes. There is no hatred in him, no recrimination. Instead he is filled with a deep sense of peace. As he brings down the cleaver in his fantasy, he finds Poltu tugging at his sleeve but ignores him. He looks at the haadikath, sees the goat's severed head and torso being taken away and the blood that has filled the middle of the courtyard.

Another goat is being dragged forward and he finds himself going into a trance again. The slender, pale neck and the two strands of silver appear again in his mind's eye. The dhakis have worked themselves up into a frenzy and the hubbub among the spectators increases. However, what he hears is a deep silence as both he and the man at the haadikath raise their cleavers together. As they come down on the waiting necks his mind seems to leave his body, rise and float away to a place of calm, of peace.

# 22

# Nausea

This is one of the few days of the year when Sohini and her mother, Bani, have dinner together. Their daily routines hardly overlap. Bani rises and sleeps early, makes it a point to have her meals on time and walks in the neighbourhood park in the morning. Sohini rises late. After an afternoon blackout, the delayed effect of the morning's alcohol and medication, that crashes on her like a monster wave, she fights a daily battle with insomnia. She usually eats the packed lunch that she carries from home but dinner comprises raids on the refrigerator and morsels of cold leftovers.

Bani spends a considerable part of her day reading and writing. She does this with a Quaker's sense of purpose and she strives hard to maintain a weekly schedule. On alternate Friday mornings, she mails the fruits of her labour

– meticulously researched essays and book reviews – in neatly addressed manila envelopes. She does not mind if an obscure academic journal or struggling little magazine publishes it. The rigour and routine keeps her ticking and she is a sprightly seventy-three. Of late she has discovered the pleasures of blogging that she does on a laptop Brinda has gifted her. It offers her the freedom that she has always wanted, the ability to write and be read almost instantly without the endless wait for a journal referee's or editor's approval.

Unlike Sohini, who rarely watches a film except on television and that too in bits and pieces, her mother remains an avid film watcher. Bani is staunch in her belief that films should be watched in a theatre. The temporary community of a film's audience, brought together in their willing suspension of reality and the common embrace of celluloid make-believe, brings her a sense of comfort. She reserves the solitary communion with the television screen for news and news only.

Thus she spends most of her Saturday afternoons in the darkness of one of the city's multiplex theatres in the company of her old college friends, munching popcorn and corn nachos that the new theatres serve in small cardboard trays. She enjoys these regular outings – the films followed by tea and sandwiches at a club. At her age she has to make the effort to live and in this she never slackens.

Among the many conflicts in their relationship, it is her

daughter's defeatism that irks her the most. In the past, Bani has entreated her to retire from the police and look for employment elsewhere and has been disappointed by her daughter's indifference. Now she isn't able to fathom why she has decided to return to the crime branch at a few hours' notice despite her ignominious exit and her shoddy treatment. She has learnt not to voice her opinions or ask the wrong questions, to avoid the fights and the emotional bruises that her interference in her daughter's life invariably leaves behind. The septuagenarian and her middle-aged daughter have worked out a formula for coexistence, not entirely happy but not wholly bitter either.

This dinner, early for Sohini and late for her mother, is a ritual they go through on her father's birthday. Bani makes the effort every year to cook some of his favourite dishes – a light mutton curry, a slightly sweet pulao with raisins, prawns in mustard followcd by a ricc pudding. Sohini is a poor catcr, a nibbler, and though she tries to compliment the chef by taking generous helpings, there is always a lot of food left on her plate at the end of these somewhat ceremonial meals.

Soumitra Sen, Sohini's father, passed away exactly twenty-four years ago, felled by a heart attack in the middle of a board meeting of the tea company where he had worked for two decades. He had been a keen student with the promise of being an astute historian whose interests lay largely in early-twentieth-century politics. Like his daughter, he had disappointed his mentors when he chose the lure of the commercial world over the drudge of academia.

The conversation at the dining table is desultory and one-sided. Bani tells her about the petty problems of their household – the gardener's truancy, the maid's spendthrift ways with the fabric softener, the seepage in the bathroom ceiling and the pending car insurance. Sohini listens patiently and occasionally offers to get her assistant Mullick or Ram Bahadur to fix a few things. She also enquires about her mother's friends and learns of Mallikamashi's uterine cancer, Belapishi's elevation to the club's food and beverage committee and her husband Priyomesho's affair with a fellow golfer, the ladies' champion of the club tournament who is half his age.

As she spoons the mutton on to her plate, she suddenly remembers the hunt for medicines in Ahona's flat and the strips of Vominix, the nausea suppressant. 'Do you remember our trips to the hills in summer?' she asks her mother. 'The way I started to puke just as the taxi left the railway station and the anxious rummage in your handbag for the green strip of Vominix. In those days, no one really cared about the right dose or the side effects and I recall popping them rather freely. There's so much fuss about these things nowadays with all the warnings about side effects and drug interactions. People like to be scared of every little thing.'

'I tend to take these things seriously,' Bani replies. 'I know you pop your sleeping pills like lozenges. I am sure that they damage your nervous system. I just wish you were a little more careful. Now that you mention Vominix, I remember Bula, Mallika's daughter, was overdosing on them for her morning sickness in the first couple of months of her pregnancy until the gynaecologist finally put a stop to it because it could affect the fetus. The medicine is specifically meant for motion sickness, not for any and every kind of nausea, but she, like you, had not bothered to read the fine print.'

Bani notices a change in Sohini. She has the fixed but puzzled stare of a Sudoku solver struggling with her last column of numbers. She has stopped eating and is drumming the table with the fingers of her left hand in a percussive and nervous rat-a-tat.

'What is it? What did I say to get you so worked up?' Bani asks.

Sohini rises from the table, pats her mother gently on the cheek and says, 'Sorry, Ma. I just remembered something very important. I have to make some calls now. Will you finish your dinner and keep the rest in the fridge? I'll eat later. I feel terrible about spoiling this one evening that we spend together but promise to make it up to you soon.'

She goes to her bedroom, locks the door and dials the family doctor, Niloy Chaudhuri. Niloy is a couple of years younger than her and one of the few doctors in the city who despite their flourishing practice bother to keep up with the rapid changes in medical science. On the few occasions that she has accompanied her mother to his clinic, she has found a copy of either the *Lancet* or the *New England Journal of Medicine*, neatly bookmarked, lying on his table.

Niloy is examining a patient but Sohini insists on speaking to him for a couple of minutes and asks him without preamble about Vominix. 'Vominix is commonly abused here by pregnant women, particularly in the first few months of pregnancy when morning sickness can be acute. An occasional pill or two is unlikely to harm the fetus but new research shows that regular use could certainly be harmful. In fact, the USFDA has issued a fairly severe warning against its misuse. There are some new drugs that we prescribe along with Vitamin B6 but I know for a fact that Vominix is still very popular,' he tells her. Then he asks rather sheepishly whether she has been experiencing these symptoms herself and mentions a competent gynaecologist friend of his that she might like to consult.

'For god's sake, Niloy, I am forty-seven and single in every sense of the word,' she admonishes him jokingly and hangs up.

She rifles through the drawer in her bedroom to find the photocopy of the forensic report. She is not interested in the medical report but in the senior forensic pathologist who signed off on the report. The signature and the name printed at the bottom confirm her suspicion. She remembers the name Sumit Bhaduri well and of the three instances of suppression of evidence that he was accused of six or seven years ago. Two of them were cases of rape and murder where Bhaduri had claimed that there was no sexual assault. She tries hard but cannot remember the third. Bhaduri had been blacklisted by the police for a year but was now back on the police roster.

The city's police association was once very active with a regular lecture series where it invited forensic experts, ballistics specialists, criminologists and senior investigators from police departments across the world. Of the many lectures she had heard, one remains etched in her memory. The speaker was a retired detective sergeant from Edinburgh and she had to strain hard to follow his thick Scots accent. He had concluded his speech with this advice to the young inductees to the crime branch:

'A case is like a jigsaw puzzle where you are handed the pieces but not shown what the puzzle looks like. The turning point comes when some of the pieces have fitted together and you are able to see a picture of the completed puzzle in your mind's eye. Then it should be easy for you to finish the rest of it. If you still find it hard to put your puzzle together there could be two possibilities. Either you've got the picture wrong or some of the pieces are missing. That's a call you have to take. At times some of the pieces will be deliberately hidden from you. Your job as a detective is to find them.'

Sohini now knows what the puzzle looks like. She knows which of the pieces are missing and also where to find them. Ahona was pregnant at the time of her murder, and was overdosing on Vominix to fight her morning sickness. She wanted to hide this fact – hence the hiding of the medicines and her strange reaction to Shefali at the pharmacy. Bhaduri had excluded this from the medical report. Shonjoy knew about this and the siblings were possibly thinking of a way to handle this unexpected exigency. Hence the rise in the frequency and duration of his calls to her.

She lies down, but doesn't bother to shut her eyes and stares at the ceiling fan. As she watches the blades rotate in their tireless endeavour, the same questions keep coming back to her in an unrelenting loop. Was Ahona really pregnant or was she imagining it all? Who was the father? Who had bribed Bhaduri to doctor the autopsy? What was the need to withhold the pregnancy? Who was the father? Would his identity take her a step forward to solving the murder? Of these many queries, one seems to gnaw at her the most. Was Shonjoy aware that his sister was pregnant or was she trying to hide it from him as well?

As she thinks of Bhaduri, she feels anger welling up in her. She cannot quite fathom where it stems from, this sense of moral outrage at the greed and deception of the pathologist, an old cog in the city's policing machine. After all, suppression of evidence is not exactly rare in investigations in this part of the world and she is hardly a naive idealist. But the anger builds, forcing her out of bed, and she paces up and down. She thinks of ways to confront Bhaduri. If she tries to interrogate him, all she is likely to get is the deception of a practised liar. She must feed this anger, let it grow and use it to win this battle.

It is well past eleven but she calls Arjun. She remembers him telling her that he would be up late to watch the semi-finals of a European football tournament. He picks up at the first ring, listens to her patiently and assures her he will meet her at Bhaduri's office at seven in the morning.

Arjun thinks it's a bad idea to confront Bhaduri. His nickname in police circles, 'gondar', that is, rhinoceros, does not refer to his physical characteristics – he is a frail man in his mid fifties – but instead to the thickness of his metaphorical hide when it comes to fending off charges of corruption, suppressing evidence and leaking information to the press for a fee. No doubt he has been blacklisted once but that was the result of a vicious turf war between him and the principal of the medical college.

Much as Arjun admires Sohini's feistiness and empathizes with her moral outrage, he is convinced that she is no match for the wily survivor. He decides to call her. But she is not dissuaded. 'Arjun, you are too timid to be a police officer,' she says jokingly. 'Go watch your silly match.'

# 23

# Undoing

Arjun can sense her rage when they meet near the staircase of Bhaduri's office in the morning. It seems to radiate like the shimmer around heated metal. It is a rage that can dissipate only after a violent eruption.

Sumit Bhaduri specialized in forensic pathology not because he was at the bottom of his class and was excluded from the more coveted specializations like cardiology or surgery. He was genuinely interested in the subject. He is still considered the best in the city, endowed with a skill that can tell of the deep waters that flowed beneath the faintest scar on a corpse or a patch on an excised liver. While his passion for forensics hasn't diminished, the inevitable regrets of middle age have long descended on him. His biggest angst stems from the size of his pay cheque. He is fifty-three and resentful of having to survive on a government salary in a crumbling government apartment with virtually nothing accumulated as a nest egg. He envies his friends who made more sensible, rewarding choices and earn more in a day than he makes in a month. While the opportunity for malfeasance, for swapping favours for hard cash, is rare in forensics, Bhaduri never lets one that occasionally comes his way slip past.

When Sohini and Arjun barge into his office at seven Bhaduri has been working for almost an hour skimming through the last bunch of toxicology reports on his table. He likes to finish his paperwork by eight after which he gets down to the grisly business of what he calls 'skinning the corpses'. A young assistant tries to stop them saying 'Sir is busy' but Sohini shoves him aside and pushes open the quaint saloon doors. Bhaduri is taken aback a little and is about to greet her when she grabs him by the collar and asks, 'Tell me, you bastard! Why did you hide the fact that Ahona was pregnant when she was murdered? Tell me now, you sisterfucker.'

She shakes Bhaduri so hard that his spectacles drop to the floor in a noisy clatter. Arjun tries to pull her back, to separate her from her victim, but is surprised by the ferocity with which she resists. The assistant rushes in to see what's happening but when Sohini screams at him and pats her waist as if to check for her gun he is quick to leave.

Bhaduri is initially too stunned to protest but soon regains his composure. The menace in his voice when he speaks to Sohini makes Arjun's skin crawl.

'Get your hands off me, Ms Sen. I have reported exactly what I found in the autopsy. I don't know from where you got the idea that Ahona was pregnant, but you are dead wrong. Perhaps the stress of the case and the years of substance abuse that *Aaj Porjonto* so correctly reported have damaged your brain. I suggest you seek medical help. But don't think you can get away with your shenanigans. You have assaulted a senior pathologist who is closely associated with the police. I will ensure that you are suspended before the day is out.'

Sohini knows she has made a mistake. She needs to retreat to her corner of the ring, give herself a little time to breathe and get back into the fight.

Arjun believes the fight is over; the match has gone to Sumit Bhaduri.

---

It is a short drive to the police station. On their way, she calls Ronen and asks to see him and Nayantara at her office in the next hour. He sounds annoyed, says he is about to leave for work, asks if it would be convenient to meet in the afternoon instead. Sohini insists, 'If you really want to help with the probe, you should come over now.'

She asks Deputy Commissioner Mukherjee's secretary if she can use his office for an hour. He is away for the day for a conference on improving IT systems in police. The secretary, Dilipbabu, is possessive of his boss's domain but after an initial reluctance gives in.

Arjun meets the Chatterjees at the gate, helps get their entry passes at the reception and, as he ushers them into Mukherjee's office, he finds Sohini seated on the boss's high-backed swivel chair, its back covered by a clean white towel. She looks more diminutive than usual.

There is no prelude to this conversation.

'Mr Chatterjee, were you aware that your daughter was pregnant?' Sohini asks.

Ronen appears surprised but his response seems so carefully rehearsed that she realizes in a matter of seconds that he has been briefed about their encounter with Bhaduri. The rest is easy to figure out. There's no need for complex deduction, just the simple yet infallible principle of common sense. Bhaduri had no reason to have met or spoken to Ronen let alone tell him about the early morning fracas unless Ronen was the one who had paid the bribe.

'I have no idea what you are talking about, Ms Sen. Ahona certainly didn't mention anything. I read the forensic report and there was nothing there. You claim that the murderer has been arrested and yet you call us here to cast aspersions on my dead daughter. What nonsense is this?'

Arjun can see a vein throbbing in Ronen's right temple and his fists are clenched. His stare reminds Arjun of a veteran pugilist, contemplating a sucker punch to end this bout with this upstart amateur, a bout that should not have been held in the first place.

'Could someone have pressured the pathologist to suppress the pregnancy?' Sohini persists.

'Are you conducting a serious investigation or living in your old little world of hunches and fantasies? Do you have any proof of this?'

Sohini turns to Nayantara. Her anger has subsided. Her question to her is an entreaty. 'Do you know anything about this?'

Nayantara's expression is inscrutable. All she says is, 'You've heard what Ronen has to say. That should put your doubts to rest.'

Sohini realizes her error of judgement, chides herself for her naivety, for believing for a moment that her anger and an imagined moral force were any match for the deviousness of those against whom they are pitted. Then she is very frightened, afraid of the consequences of her recklessness. She knows Arjun is disappointed in her, maybe even disgusted, fearful of the penalties that his association with her will bring to his career as a cop.

Ronen is ready with his parting shot. 'I was instrumental in involving you in this investigation,' he says. 'It was obviously a mistake. Your long exile from the crime branch has taken a toll on your abilities as an investigator. You should get some rest and get the case reassigned to someone else. Can we leave now or are there more of these fantasies that you want to share with us?'

As her fear subsides and she can think more clearly, a flurry of questions enters her mind, questions to which she has no quick answers however hard she thinks. She tries to organize them in a sequence, ducks in a neat row, hoping that some logical train will emerge that will bring her to a denouement.

She can understand a father's anxiety to protect his dead child's reputation. But in this case, his deception would compromise his own daughter's murder. Had he killed her then? Hired someone to do it for him?

A stream of disjointed, random memories follows. Scenes of different films cut and pasted together in a crazy sequence by an editor on a mind-bending drug. Shonjoy's expression on the first day they met him at his parents' house. The snigger in Atreyi's voice as she described her husband's obsessive fondness for his sister. Nayantara's loud and angry blaming of Ronen for their daughter's murder. Ahona's counsellor hinting that she might well have been afraid of someone in her family. Maya's halting, shame-filled account of her ward's sexual obsession. Brutus, the family dog, stabbed by a deranged teenager.

Intuition follows, uniting these discrete memories, telling her a story, guiding her to a conclusion. Ronen was neither the killer nor the father of the unborn child. The father was

Shonjoy. He was shielding his son. Was the son his sister's killer then?

---

In the afternoon, she gets a call from an unknown number. The caller is Ambika Tripathy, Bhaduri's petrified assistant whom they had met in the morning. He wants to meet them but wants to keep the meeting secret. They agree to meet at the coffee house.

Ambika is a thin, fidgety man in his late twenties with a marked stammer. His medical degrees are from a northern university and his job at Bhaduri's laboratory is his first.

'It's a contract job. I am not a proper government servant,' he says wistfully.

As soon as they are seated at a corner table, he launches into a tirade against his boss. His stock of phrases is limited and he keeps repeating 'bad man' over and over again. They know much of what he is saying – Bhaduri's venality, his willingness to fudge forensic reports if a bid meets his ask and his shoddy treatment of his juniors.

'He even demands a cut of our bonus,' Tripathy whines.

'Is there something specific you want to tell us?' she asks.

She is hardly surprised when he tells her. 'Ms Chatterjee was carrying a baby when she was killed. I was part of the autopsy team. I saw the fetus myself. Must have been two months old. There is more. We found scars on the uterus that were likely caused by abortions in the past.'

Sohini remembers her conversation with Shefali, the niggling illnesses and the occasional surgeries. Except that they weren't for polyps in her uterus; she was terminating her pregnancies.

'Do you know who bribed Bhaduri to doctor the report?' Sohini asks.

'Not exactly. But Bhaduri has become quite brazen about these things. He doesn't think I even exist. I heard him on the phone saying, "Ronenbabu, you shouldn't worry when I am there."'

'Why are you telling us this? What's in it for you?' Arjun asks.

'I need madam's help with a transfer to another hospital. I cannot bear to work another day with Bhaduri sir. I know madam knows people in the CM's office. If she puts in a word, I will be transferred in a day.'

'Will you say this in front of the commissioner when I meet him tomorrow?'

'Whatever you say, madam.'

She gets the call she has been dreading from the commissioner's office. He would like to see her and Arjun the next morning at nine sharp. She calls Tripathy, who promises to be there.

# 24

# The Natural Order

Sohini believes that an attempt to suppress critical evidence would give her enough reason to take Ronen and Shonjoy into temporary police custody. She wants to question them separately, check for inconsistencies in their responses, play one against the other, batter them with accusations till the sheer fatigue of denial and dissembling cracks their defence. But first she needs to prove that the autopsy report was indeed tampered with, evidence suppressed. She knows she is clutching at a solitary straw, the promise made by a terrified young man from a small town to go against his boss, to summon the courage and bet on her ability to get him a transfer. She has her doubts but hasn't abandoned hope altogether.

Arjun believes in a natural order of things in which people like him and Ambika are underlings, whose dharma is to obey unquestioningly, not to disrupt this order. He also has a grudging admiration for Bhaduri's ability to survive any onslaught on his career and reputation. He does not share Sohini's hope.

As they walk down the long corridor that leads to the commissioner's office, they are both silent and lost in their thoughts. She steals a glance at Arjun and knows he has given up the fight. She thinks of her future if Tripathy lets her down – her brief resurrection as a working cop solving crimes soon over, banished again to an obscure department, a useless pen-pusher surviving at the edges of the state bureaucracy.

Sohini is surprised to find Sumit Bhaduri seated next to Ambika in the small waiting room adjoining the commissioner's office. Arjun, however, had expected this. The pathologists are ushered into the room along with the detectives.

The commissioner wants to keep this meeting brief. He is running late for a meeting with the home secretary. His reprimand is terse and precise.

'Ms Sen, Dr Bhaduri wishes to lodge a formal complaint against you for assaulting him yesterday. I have requested him not to put it on record on the condition that I take appropriate action against you. I hope you appreciate the fact that we cannot let these things happen in the force. He happens to be the senior-most pathologist in the city.'

'But have you heard Tripathy's side of the story?' she asks tentatively.

'I have, Ms Sen. I am honestly shocked that you didn't stop at assaulting Dr Bhaduri. You tried to intimidate his junior assistant to give false evidence against him. That incidentally is part of the complaint that they want to lodge against you. Gentlemen, I would request you to reconsider your decision. Would you take a day to think about it, please? Now if you will excuse me, I have something to discuss with Ms Sen and Arjun.'

Sohini looks at Ambika Tripathy. Their eyes meet for a moment before he averts his gaze. She feels neither anger nor contempt for him. Instead she is overcome by a deep sense of pity.

As the pathologist and his assistant leave, Commissioner Banerjee continues in his businesslike manner. 'You are both off the case as of now. You will hand over the files to Dipayan, who will take charge himself. No, I am not suspending you, Ms Sen. You will take a few weeks' leave and return to the crime branch. I remember how the media turned you into a martyr, a victim of police corruption and politics, after you botched up the Sethia case. I will not allow that to happen again. You may go now.'

As she walks out alone through the heavy wooden doors, her first impulse is to rush to her office, switch the computer on, type out a resignation letter and hand it to the commissioner. However, as she walks back down the long corridor and climbs the two flights of stairs to her shared office, she calms down. The events of yesterday have taught her a lesson about the perils of haste. She calls Ram Bahadur instead; she wants him to drive her to the riverfront.

Arjun, who has just entered the office, insists on going with her. She tries to dissuade him. 'Don't worry, Arjun,' she says with a weak smile, 'I won't jump into the river. At least not immediately.' But he is adamant.

They buy the cheap entry tickets to the promenade and find an empty bench. It is almost noon and the sun is out. However, the winds have changed shift as winter approaches. There is a breeze blowing down the river from the sea a couple of hundred kilometres to the south and they can bear the heat. They sit silently at opposite ends of the bench and stare at the muddy brown water. Both seem to believe that there is peace to be found in the constancy of the river, the fact that it will persevere in carrying its water to the sea undisturbed by the vagaries of the lives of the city and its dwellers.

---

But the saga doesn't end here. This is an impatient city, a streetfighting city used to punches, bruises and screams till it gets what it wants. It certainly won't take the murder of a young woman in its own backyard lying down. The opposition party led by Tarok Panda, the newspapers, the television channels and the army of amateur opinion-makers on the social media want a head on the pike. The chief minister, Subhendubabu and Commissioner Banerjee decide to give them one.

Raju Mahto had been released from police custody but was kept under careful watch. A charge sheet is hastily prepared and Durga Maity's note on his conclusion that the killer was right-handed removed. Raju is arrested and put behind bars, an undertrial with the distracted legal counsel of an overworked young pro-bono lawyer.

For three days shots of Raju being hoisted into the police van by two burly constables, face hidden by a green towel, make it to the headlines of every television channel. The most poignant images, however, are of his calloused fingers clutching the wire mesh of the van's window as if he is holding on to the last vestiges of life as a free man.

A number of television channels visit his village. His father sounds categorical when he speaks to the swarm of black microphones that are thrust into his face. 'He is a drug addict and a killer,' he says. 'We have nothing to do with him. Shiv Pujan is no longer our son.' He does not allow the reporters to speak to his wife, who is heard weeping copiously inside their hut.

# 25

# Addiction

**Twelve years ago**

This is his third kill and the easiest to cover his tracks. This town is in the middle of a riot. Bodies hacked, burnt to char. The police are too preoccupied to bother with the finer nuances of this crime, nuances that make it different from the wanton butchery on the streets. The curfew is over but he has been stopped twice by gun-toting policemen, their hands trembling, crazed by the carnage that they see around. He has flashed his ID card and the guns have been lowered, apologies tendered.

He had thought that his first killing would bring finality to his quest but that was not to be. There is always a regression, a pushing back from the finishing line, and he needs to push forward again, find new prey and bring his cleaver down with just the right velocity. He knows his technique is not yet perfect. The blade should be slicing all the way through. Perhaps it is a flaw in his instrument of death. But he finds a growing attachment to his cleaver and to the position he takes behind the trussed-up body, the firm grip of his left hand on the clump of hair at the nape. These have become markers of his very own unique ritual. So have the gloves, the crude polythene socks, the cook's hairnet to thwart a stray strand of hair, the nakedness. He used them first as a foil to the forensic investigator's trained eye – no finger- or footprints, no bloodstained clothes fished out from a dump. Now they bring him a strange pleasure – the disrobing, the tightness of the latex on his fingers, the squelch of polythene on a puddle of blood.

He suspects that his need to kill has morphed from a spiritual quest to an addiction. He needs a hit of this drug, needs to feel the course of the blood in his veins accelerate, the slight agitation in his heart and brain before he soars. Like all addictions, this too has a progression, even if non-linear. The craving for another hit comes sooner, is more intense and the withdrawal is worse. He has learnt to handle the withdrawal, to shoot up drugs into his veins till the shakes, the itchiness and the flutter in his mind stop. But these just alleviate the symptom like pills taken for a cold. The sniffles cease for a while but the virus remains.

# 26

# Hiatus

Sohini stays on in the crime branch and takes three weeks' leave. She visits Sajal in Goa, walks on the beach but as far from the waves as possible. They remind her of yet another of her many failures. Despite the meticulous plans of suicide she had made in the armchair comfort of her dark, shuttered living room, she simply doesn't have the courage to end it all. She thinks that she is born to be a survivor, a word she abhors, a word that connotes a life of compromise and mute acceptance. A survivor like a limpet or an iguana, an ugly thing with a suction device stuck to its feet that keeps it from falling even as it moves steadily down a rock face.

What bothers her most is the realization that she and Sumit Bhaduri are not so different after all. Both have thick hides; she is as much of a gondar as him. Otherwise she would have slapped her resignation down on the commissioner's table. The only difference is that Bhaduri has been able to play this game of survival more successfully.

There is another thing that rankles, keeps her on the balcony of the guest house at night instead of the comfort of the pull-out bed in her room, staring at the twinkling lights of the ships far out in the sea, eluded by sleep despite the heavy-liddedness in her eyes that her pills and the many glasses of rum bring on. She chides herself for being used, played like a cheap puppet at a poor man's fair. She realizes that Ronen deliberately chose her – a failed cop – so that if something came out about Shonjoy she might feel obligated to help her benefactor or if she turned out to be intransigent Ronen could have her discredited easily enough.

Another realization that strikes her is that her drinking is out of control. Once she returns to the city, she starts attending AA meetings in a run-down community hall once owned by the Freemasons. The masons are long gone and the disputed property is under court receivership. She takes her pledge in the company of a motley crowd, everyone grim and resolute. Some of them claim to have been off the bottle for months and seem proud of their little victories, their badges of honour. The visible tremors in their hands tell Sohini that their battle for sobriety is far from won.

She stays sober for a few days, but when the self-loathing gets the better of her, she goes on a bender. She drinks at home, passes out on her armchair and wakes with a killer of a crick in her neck and a blinding headache. When she finds the cushion that her mother had carefully placed beneath her head and the light sheet she has covered her with, she cries uncontrollably. It makes her headache worse.

During the day, she tries to read, to draw solace from the writers who comforted her in her youth. She sticks to short stories, her power of concentration is too tattered to attempt a novel. She reads Alice Munro, Salinger and Manik Bandopadhyay, stories with unexpected and often sad, devastating endings. This gives her a temporary succour as do her tapes of Western classical music that she plays on her old boom box with its faulty rewind button.

On a brisk October morning she returns to the crime branch, finds she has a tiny new office and spends her first day immersed in a fat compilation of Sudoku puzzles. She finds she can fill some of the rows and columns but a full puzzle is way beyond her abilities. Arjun stops by and talks about his new assignment, a desk job helping catalogue the branch's archives and transfer them to a computer with the help of a pimply faced IT consultant.

Her first week is spent avoiding her colleagues' stares, turning a deaf ear to their whispers and letting their barbs ricochet off her gondar hide.

---

It takes a month for her to get a case. She investigates an alleged arson in a warehouse next to the large wholesale market in the north of the city. She likes the young, efficient woman who works alongside, Swapna, the insurance claims investigator. Both of them unearth a complex insurance fraud. Commissioner Banerjee calls to congratulate her and she is so happy with this small gesture of approbation that she starts to weep.

Her mind refuses to jettison Ahona's case altogether and on a couple of evenings every week she finds herself tailing Shonjoy Chatterjee's car, like a dogged paparazzo in search of a scandal, on his long, solitary drives on the riverfront. She drives her small Korean hatchback herself on these evenings but her pursuit is futile. Shonjoy drives up and down for about an hour and returns home.

---

Three months later she is surprised to get a call from Atreyi. She sounds afraid and wants to meet her as soon as possible. She has separated from Shonjoy and lives in a small flat near her bank. Sohini meets her there. She looks different, haggard, her hauteur gone, a pleading look on her face.

'I have been getting threatening calls asking me to leave the city. I have always wanted to leave but my mother has cancer and she trusts the doctors here. My brothers are in Raipur and Gwalior and the medical facilities aren't as good. Ms Sen, you'll have to promise to help me.'

'Do you have some idea of who is behind this?'

'My father-in-law was very keen that both Shonjoy and I leave the city even before he heard of our decision to separate. I think he is particularly keen to see me gone.'

'Can you think of a reason?'

She waits for a moment before telling her.

'I overheard a conversation that I was not meant to hear. It confirmed what I had always suspected. Ronen found me eavesdropping.'

---

It's the evening of Ahona's cremation. She is at the Chatterjee residence compiling a list of guests for the prayer meeting. She walks towards her mother-in-law's bedroom to get it vetted. She can hear Nayantara, her husky voice straining to keep low.

'...that's how much you know your children, Ronen. You were not even aware that she was pregnant until that gold-digger pathologist told you. That your beloved son had fathered his sister's child for the third time. This time when she got pregnant she came to me. She wanted to keep the baby, kept telling me that this was her last chance to have a child. The poor girl thought that if she went through another abortion, she wouldn't be able to conceive ever again. She hid her morning sickness pills just to make sure that Shonjoy or you wouldn't find out about the baby when you visited.'

She continues, her voice getting raspier as she lights a cigarette. 'You think you cared for your children and I didn't. You just bought their affection, bought it cheap. Your sex-crazed son knocks up your daughter twice and all you do is get her an abortion and send her to a silly psychiatrist who pumps her with pills and spends an hour with her every week playing Freud. Of course they hated me because I would have been tougher, stopped all that nonsense before it got completely out of hand.'

The door knob turns suddenly and Atreyi finds herself facing Ronen.

---

This is hard evidence. For a moment Sohini thinks she can reopen Ahona's case, take Atreyi to the commissioner's office to tell him this story. Then she hears Atreyi telling her, 'Listen to me please, Ms Sen, I beg of you. Whatever you can do to help, leave the commissioner out of it. He is close to Ronen and I won't be surprised if he knows about these threats.'

'Try not to worry. I will speak to Arjun and get some of the junior officers to see what can be done. Call me whenever you need to.'

---

Six months pass. Commissioner Banerjee goes on yet another secondment, this time to Manila. Anish Lall, a star cop on lien to the Intelligence Bureau in Delhi for the past three years, is brought back to his home cadre to replace him. Anish, a physics graduate from one of Delhi's elite colleges, is a year senior to Sohini and knows her well. He is an Anglophile and after spending a decade in the police took a sabbatical at the London School of Economics reading politics. When Sohini was removed from the crime branch, Lall was away. She remembers the cryptic text message from him, written in his inimitable caricature of a toff. It said, 'Chin up, old girl.'

Lall gives Sohini more cases and occasionally calls her to his office to seek her counsel. He needs allies to survive the vicious internal politics of the crime branch, its daily skirmishes over turf and territory, the jousting of egos in a top-heavy department. Soon, Sohini is branded a card-carrying member of the Lall camp.

---

It's been almost eight months since Ahona's murder, Raju Mahto's trial date has been postponed twice at the request of the prosecution and the murdered woman almost forgotten except by her family, close friends and the two detectives.

On a late May morning, as the city reels under a heat wave made worse by a sapping humidity, Sohini and Arjun are summoned to Anish Lall's office. He wants them to investigate a murder that took place the previous evening in the district town of Lalmati, roughly two hundred kilometres west of the city. A young woman has been murdered. She is from the city but was visiting her aunt for a few days. The local police is convinced it is a simple case of robbery that turned violent when the woman resisted.

However, the Lalmati residents don't trust their local cops. This lack of trust apparently stems from an altercation over the custodial death of a teenager that the police claim was suicide. The local legislator has requested the city's crime branch to help with the investigation. 'Arjun is perfectly capable of handling this on his own. But I want Sohini to be involved because the legislator expects a senior officer. He is quite powerful in the party,' Lall explains.

Sohini has piles of paperwork to finish. The entire police apparatus in the city is being restructured with the help of an American consulting firm. There are job profiles to be described in minute detail, flow charts to be drawn and PowerPoint presentations prepared. Young men in blue suits and muted pastel ties are swarming all over the crime branch headquarters. She tells Arjun to go on his own this morning; she will go later.

# 27

# Lalmati

Lalmati is an old jute mill town to the west of the city. Its economy once thrived around the Laxmi Jute Mill, owned by the Aggarwal family. The mill's fortunes started ebbing with the decline of jute hessian as packing material as synthetic upstarts started to gnaw at its markets. It made a valiant attempt to survive by diversifying into other products like carpets and jute textiles. However, a militant trade union and the cut-throat sweatshop economics of Bangladeshi producers ensured that its resuscitation was brief. By the mid nineties the factory had shut down, leaving the local economy in ruins.

Lalmati, literally red earth, gets its name from the ferrous content of its soil though geologists have long pointed out that the percentage of iron in the soil is too low for any serious mining. In fact the soil in Lalmati is not the rich red of the mining belts that lie a few hundred kilometres to the south and west. The colour is best described as tawny, a dirty orange brown.

---

Usha Jain, twenty-five years old, has been murdered in what was once the guest house of the mill. It is a sprawling bungalow with a garden and is right on the bank of the river. It is now private property and belongs to Geeta Pachisia, the widow of Ramdeo Pachisia who was the general manager of the mill. Usha was their niece.

Having spent three decades of his life in Lalmati, Ramdeo decided to stay on after the mill shut down and bought the guest house from the Aggarwals at a fire-sale price. The spaciousness of the house, the garden with its thickets of pink and white bougainvillea and the view of the river compensated for its isolation and the eeriness of the ghostly ruins of the jute factory right next door. Besides, Lalmati town was a short drive away, daily provisions were available there, and a retinue of servants ensured that life was comfortable.

When Ramdeo died of a heart attack five years ago, the economics of the household changed, despite the shares and debentures he had left behind. As Geeta's arthritis progressed from being just a fleeting pain in the joints on damp mornings to a disease that virtually crippled her, her medical bills inflated. The retinue of servants dwindled down to Ramu, who stayed during the day, and Sarala, who came from a neighbouring village in the evening and stayed the night. Sarala had come down with dengue three days ago and Usha had come all the way from the city to look after her ailing aunt.

This, in a nutshell, was what Sub-inspector Shyamal Ghosh of Lalmati police station had gleaned from his long interview with a distraught Ramu and Mrs Pachisia. He shares this with Arjun as he drives him from the station to the Pachisia residence.

'You needn't have bothered to come,' Ghosh tells him. 'This is a simple robbery that went out of hand. Mrs Jain's gold mangalsutra and her laptop and phone that were on the dining table are gone. She was killed in the living room. The Jain woman had locked the door that led to the bedrooms and kept the key in a drawer of the desk. Apparently this was the regular arrangement when she wanted to stay up and watch TV and her aunt went to sleep. The assailant must have asked her for it. She must have refused and so he tied and gagged her and tried looking for it himself. When he couldn't find it, he must have used his sickle on her neck. The aunt was inside all the time, screaming her lungs out. He must have panicked and left with whatever he had laid his hands on.

'This is not a fancy city murder, Arjunbabu,' he continues. 'You have to understand the people who live here to get to the nub of things. Some of them are so poor that they would kill for a ballpoint pen. Have you heard of Bournvita, Mr Sinha?'

Before Arjun can answer, Ghosh continues his monologue. 'It's not the fancy health drink that obese kids drink in the city. It's local hooch, so strong that you will start flying when you have your first gulp. They put industrial chemicals in it; it comes in a small plastic pouch. But once you get used to it, it makes you hyperactive for a few hours and when the effect wears off you fall into a hole. The locals are addicted to it. Some of the NGO people who try to help the addicts' families tell me that one of the side effects could be a propensity for violence. I can bet my life's savings that the killer was on the stuff. Besides, a sickle is the easiest thing to get hold of. There are dozens lying around on every farm. Posh city cops like you think we need your fancy forensics but I can assure you that my team of yokels will catch the killer in the next forty-eight hours. We have a list of local criminals and now just need to round them up and give them the third degree. Someone will talk.'

—

The spectators, drawn from nearby villages, have dutifully gathered at the mill. They look both curious and a little frightened, stopped at the factory complex gate by the police. News evidently travels fast here. A few television vans are parked there and Arjun notices some familiar faces of journalists from Ahona's crime scene.

The guest house has a separate entrance through a driveway. Compared to the derelict factory with some of the machinery lying outside like exhibits in a postmodern art museum, the bungalow looks well maintained. However, the current occupant's diminished financial status is visible in the cracks in its concrete exterior and the large patches of moss on the walls that cry out for a coat of paint. Someone seems to tend the garden, but half-heartedly. Four flower beds with some flowers in bloom mark a sharp contrast to the thick, uncut grass of the lawn and the weeds that vie for space.

Arjun and Shyamal Ghosh enter the living room, where Usha's body was found, bound and gagged. It is large, almost like a small auditorium with a massive sofa set with faded upholstery and a scratched coffee table that badly needs to be polished. There are two large but threadbare carpets with ornate Kashmiri designs and a dining table that seats eight, relics from a more fortunate age for the mill. A writing desk sits next to a door that presumably leads to the bedrooms. The cloying smell of mildew from the damp walls mixes with the smell of blood and the mild stench of early decay of the corpse. Arjun feels the first gag of nausea.

The corpse is covered with a white sheet. Despite the best efforts of the police to keep them away, flies have settled on the sheet. The blood is congealing and there are two large rust-coloured patches on the sheet like the wings of a moth. A young constable lifts the sheet.

Arjun feels a kick in his gut so strong that he imagines it coming from a large horse, the kind that he has seen the mounties of the city's force ride into a riot. The position of the body, the tied hands, the gag, the bowed head are eerily similar to the way Ahona was found.

Arjun fishes out his phone, switches on the camera, goes close to the body, shuts his eyes and starts clicking randomly, hoping that he will capture all possible angles. DCM needs to see these photographs. He then runs to the garden and keeps vomiting till he thinks that he will puke out his entrails.

Five minutes later he has recovered somewhat but is still crouching next to one of the flower beds. There is a hand on his shoulder and he hears Shyamal Ghosh's voice. 'How are you feeling now? You have a city gut, Sinha sir. Villagers like us are used to these sights.'

---

Arjun wants to speak to Usha's aunt. Ramu escorts him to her bedroom. She is in deep shock but is able to speak.

'I can't move around much because of my arthritis. I have a walking frame and if Ramu or Sarala helps me get out of bed, I can just about make it to the bathroom. I retire early and if I can't get to sleep, I read the Gita or the Hanuman

Chalisa. My door remains shut at night and Sarala sleeps on the floor.

'Usha slept next to me but she used to turn in much later. She was in the living room watching television last evening. Both my bedroom and the living room doors were closed. Usha kept coming in to check if I was all right but she always locked the door behind her and put the key in the desk drawer. There is some jewellery and a little cash in the cupboard here. One can't be too careful in this godforsaken place.

'I had dozed off when the bell rang. This must have been half an hour after Ramu left. About fifteen minutes later I thought I heard a moan but you know at my age the mind begins to play tricks on you. I called out for Usha a couple of times and when she didn't come, I felt worried. A helpless cripple like me has to learn to be patient. After waiting for about an hour, I recited my Chalisa, took two sleeping pills and went to sleep hoping I would wake up in the morning to find her sleeping next to me. Ramu has a key and he came in at around seven and told me what had happened...' And then she starts weeping.

As Arjun leaves, he sees Joyonto, a young crime scene investigator from the city's forensic team, enter. Joyonto salutes but Arjun is so deeply immersed in his thoughts that he only manages to acknowledge this with a distracted half-wave. A white Honda City drives in through the gate. He sees the face of a young man sitting in the back seat. He looks distraught, haggard. Arjun presumes it is the victim's husband but doesn't want to talk to him now.

---

Arjun insists that Sohini accompany him when they visit Usha Jain's apartment the next morning. It is in one of the new blocks that have recently come up on the southern fringes of the city, tall, toylike towers, their incongruity with the green soggy marshland that surrounds them enhanced by the bright poster colours that they are painted in. The Jains live on the eighth floor.

Mrs Jain, Usha's mother-in-law, wails loudly while her husband tries to pacify her. 'I have lost a daughter, not a daughter-in-law,' she keeps repeating. 'We shouldn't have let her go to Lalmati.' There is something about these overt displays of grief that always puts Sohini on her guard, makes her suspect that these are just a charade to conceal a lack of genuine sorrow.

Hemant, the husband who looks boyish but Sohini guesses is in his early thirties, is quiet, and looks genuinely distraught. Sohini asks if they could speak privately.

They stand in the balcony as they talk, taking in the haphazard sprawl of the city separated from them by the smooth green of the marshes, pocked here and there by the white circular nets of the small 'fisheries' that offer a safe haven for spawn from the toxic river.

'I am sorry for your loss,' Sohini forces herself to say. 'I don't mean to be callous but it's quite likely that the local police is right, that it is a case of robbery and murder that they can handle better. But I still need to ask you some questions. Where were you on the night of the murder?'

'I have a small plastics business,' he replies. 'Our factory is in the suburbs but a couple of big buyers are based in Ranchi. I had gone there day before and came back yesterday. My plane had just landed when I got a call from someone in the crime branch.'

'Did Usha go to Lalmati often?'

'No, not recently. When she visited earlier, I used to insist that she return at night. She went this time because of her aunt's illness. It was an emergency.'

'Can you think of anyone who might want to harm your wife or your family in this gruesome way?'

'I can't. We have had trouble with some of our workers at the factory but I just can't imagine anyone…'

'We will have to call you to the station at some point. Don't leave the city without checking with me.'

Hemant's parents have retired to their bedroom when they leave. Sohini can still hear his mother's wail and his father's desperate plea.

'You have to be strong, Rekha. You have to be strong.'

# 28

# Photographs

When she returns to her office in the afternoon after a hurried lunch at the canteen she finds DCM waiting for her. She can sense the excitement in him and a palpable eagerness to share it with someone.

'I apologize for having invited myself in like this. There are a couple of things that you need to see right away. I have asked Arjun to come here. I hope you don't mind. I should have taken your permission.'

'Since when did you become so formal, Durgababu?' she replies. 'There is no need to apologize.'

As Arjun walks in DCM fishes out a set of photographs from his pocket. They seem freshly printed, and from the splatter of crimson on them, she guesses they are from the previous day's crime scene.

'You have a very high resolution camera in your phone,

Arjun,' he says. 'Must have spent quite a packet on it. Never suspected you were keen on gadgets. The photographs have been taken somewhat randomly. I will not embarrass you by asking if you had your eyes shut when you took them. Not to worry though. You did a good job – managed to get shots of the severed neck from almost every possible angle.'

'Madam,' he addresses Sohini, 'I got the clerk at the archives to fish out photographs of Ahona Chatterjee's murder scene and compared the two. I know what you'll say. It is possible that a different killer might have gone through the same steps of hitting Mrs Jain on the head, tying and gagging her before striking her on the neck. However, the similarities in the MO are so stark that I am willing to bet my life's savings it is the same killer. I will repeat what I told you eight months ago.'

He continues, 'The killer goes through the same steps of preparing the victim for the kill and uses the exact same position and stroke to sever the neck. This is either part of a ritual or a pattern that he has fallen into over many killings.'

Sohini wants to ask a question but DCM doesn't pause.

'Just give me a couple of minutes more, madam. I know we can't be certain of it until the post-mortem is formally done. From whatever I could make out from the photographs, the blow to the neck was not made by a curved weapon like a sickle. I emailed the photographs to Shonali. You know Shonali Jana, don't you? She is one of the best young forensic pathologists that we have in the city. She concurred with me. Mrs Jain was murdered with a weapon that had a much straighter blade, possibly a cleaver. Again, I am willing to risk my entire professional reputation on the claim that both women were beheaded by the same kind of weapon.'

Sohini feels a rush of adrenaline, the slight numbness in her limbs as it courses through her body, the sudden burst of concentrated energy that it triggers. It is a feeling that she has become unfamiliar with. She has put up with the home guards, the dud cases, the paperwork, the dreariness of maintenance policing for this rush, the promise of a chase, like an upper that in the tick of a moment takes all the fatigue and numbness away, makes life worth living. Yet she wills herself to remain calm. She will keep her cards close to her chest this time.

'Durgababu, even if I were to concede that it was the work of a serial killer, where do I go hunting for him? Linking the two murders would mean reopening the Ahona Chatterjee case. But that's done and dusted. We have a killer behind bars. I am not questioning your professional abilities, but isn't there a tiny chance that it was a local criminal who used a cleaver instead of a sickle? Let sleeping dogs lie, Mr Maity.'

'It's your call, madam, but I would request you to keep an open mind after you see the post-mortem report. All I can offer is my support and the little expertise I have. We have worked together in this branch for almost twenty years. If I know you at all, you are quite capable of getting not just the Chatterjee case but many more cases reopened if it will help you get closer to the truth. Oh yes, I need to show you something else.'

He picks out a photograph from the pile. 'In his shooting frenzy Arjun got some shots of Mrs Jain's arm. There is a shot of her lower left arm that is fairly clear.'

He points to her wrist in the photograph.

'There is a scar on her left wrist going across her vein. Shonali thinks it's quite fresh, not more than six months old. This is what I would call a textbook scar. She had slit her wrist. You know what I am saying, don't you? She tried to kill herself recently.'

---

The city's crime branch is collaborating with the Lalmati police in Usha Jain's murder investigation. A murder victim's recent suicide attempt needs to be investigated further. She debates whether to wait for the formal post-mortem report or to question the Jains based on DCM and Dr Jana's analysis of the photograph. The post-mortem is being done at the Lalmati government hospital. It will take at least a couple of days for the report to arrive.

In a probe like this, two days is long, long enough to tamper with reports, fake alibis, bribe witnesses and derail the investigation. She decides not to take that risk and calls Hemant and his father to her office that afternoon.

'It's urgent,' she says on the phone. 'I expect you in my office in the next hour.'

When they arrive in less than an hour, she decides to be brusque, doesn't bother to ask them to sit. When they remain standing, Arjun who is seated behind her points to the chairs.

'Don't you think you should have mentioned your wife's suicide attempt to us?' she asks. 'Don't look so puzzled,' she continues. 'We saw the scar on her wrist and the doctor told us it was recent. Usha has been brutally murdered. If you are so selective in what you tell us, don't blame me if you find yourself behind bars. Besides, suicide attempts are a police matter. You paid someone off at the hospital not to report this.'

This routine works and there is both a tremor and a note of penitence in the senior Mr Jain's voice as he replies. 'We come from a conservative, close-knit community. They would ostracize us if they found out about the suicide attempt. We run a small business and depend on their support for a number of things. That includes financial help when things get a little rough. We all thought it would be in everyone's interest if it remained secret.'

'You obviously don't think your dead daughter-in-law's interest counts,' she retorts.

Mr Jain continues, 'Usha was terribly depressed after her two miscarriages. We took her to a psychiatrist for her illness. She was under treatment when she decided to take this extreme step. Fortunately, Hemant found her before it was too late. She went back to the doctor after the incident and I felt that she was recovering. She certainly looked happier.'

'When did she attempt suicide and where was she treated? I also want the names of her gynaecologist and her psychiatrist.'

'About five months ago.' He gives her a date. 'Our entire family is covered by a plan that Blue Cross Hospital offers. It is…'

'I know where the hospital is. The doctors' names please?'

'Her gynaecologist was Anita Sharma and Dr Sen was her psychiatrist. Arunava Sen. But he was at a different clinic, Alpha Clinic.'

A small shard of memory floats back into her mind. Yes, she remembers. Dr Sen was treating Ahona Chatterjee before he handed over her case to the new psychiatrist from Chennai. She remembers the conversation in his clinic, even the painting of the Rialto bridge but can't recall his name.

Arjun has seen too many cases of young brides being brutally beaten and burnt to death for not satisfying their in-laws' greed for dowry to take the Jains' explanation at face value. He wants to investigate further. Sohini agrees. 'Let's meet at Blue Cross tomorrow at eight sharp.'

# 29

# Seeking

**Twenty-eight years ago**

He finds himself in a northern city next to a river that has been held sacred for millennia. It is known for the ghats that flank its side, and the steps and the platforms that constitute them are places where devotion and commerce mingle. There are flower sellers, small kiosks from where priests offer their services and astrologers promise a glimpse of the future. Sinewy boatmen throng the lower steps of each ghat, peddling joyrides or a more purposeful row across to the bank opposite.

The search that has brought him here is not a spiritual whimsy or an affectation that will pass once he finds other distractions. He wants release from the unshakeable restlessness that fills his mind every waking moment, and respite from the vicious nightmares that jolt him awake in the early hours of the morning but fade quickly, leaving behind a residue that addles his brain like the delirium of a high fever.

What he needs is a guide, someone to help him navigate, someone who knows the path that has an end. The boilerplate motions of devotion that he sees around him at the pujas that his aunt unerringly invites him to, the cut fruits of the prasad offered to the deities, the annual calendar of fasts and feasts, the chanting of the mantras leave him unmoved.

He has believed for a while that there are other ways of seeking. When the torment has become unbearable, he has tortured himself. Like a mourner at Muharram whipping his back with an improvised whip made of rope till he has fainted or piercing himself with a hook like a charak at Chaitra Sankranti, all in the hope that the searing pain in his body will somehow cancel the pain in his soul. But nothing has worked.

When he turned to a tantric priest, a friend's uncle, he discovered that the priest's spiritual path is as much about an unquestioning adherence to rituals as his aunt's pujas. He hated the passivity of it, the blind faith in an undefined, divine munificence that will come one day. Gifts and devotion offered as a transaction, a quid pro quo where god will keep his side of the bargain.

They are difficult to find, this sect he is looking for in this northern city. The Aghoris. Their beliefs and practices are on the extreme periphery of his religion; they are feared but also deeply revered. He hasn't found much to read on them but the little research he has done has convinced him that they know the way to a place of calm, a place to drop anchor.

His rickshaw driver Kanhaiya turns out to be a procurer who offers him women, booze, ganja, charas and bhang but is visibly scared when he tells him of the 'high' he is looking for. But money talks and as he bids higher he can see the greed in Kanhaiya's eyes. There is always a price where a market is made, demand equals supply and a deal is struck. Kanhaiya accepts his final bid and agrees to leave him near a small cremation ground.

As he enters their lair in a corner of the burning ground, he is prepared for a stream of curses, even a violent encounter. He is surprised to get neither; instead, there is a terse nod from one of them to follow him. He is smeared with white ash that makes his teeth appear yellower than they actually are, and he carries both a trident and the reek of strong cheap liquor that almost overpowers him.

From the moment he meets the other sadhus who form part of this small sect, he knows he will never be accepted into their fold. They think of him as a dilettante whose curiosity is the passing fad of a spoilt city kid. However, his persistence works to a degree. Over the next few weeks they let him watch their rituals and even participate. He senses a grudging admiration – his complete absence of fear when he watches them meditate deep in the night seated on an abandoned corpse, the fact that he does not squirm when he hears their guarded tales of intercourse with the dead, of the powers that their flesh can bestow.

Rangababa is the most silent of them, always in the shadows, and watches him from a distance. When he finally speaks after a week, he is surprised to find it is in a clipped Bengali accent. 'You seem like an intelligent young man. I don't know what brought you to us, to seek this path to truth. All I can hope is that you can see beyond the fear our rituals invoke, the so-called black magic we practise. We seek the divine in ourselves, break all the taboos that the world imposes on us. Once you are free of those shackles, free of all the fear and the revulsion that you are taught to feel, you will find true happiness and freedom inside yourself. If you are always afraid to swim across the moat, how will you reach the fortress that stands within?'

He tries to spend more time with this new teacher. Rangababa is moody, lapses into hours and even days of silence. But when he speaks, there is sharpness in his expositions, a luminescent intelligence that holds him in thrall.

He speaks to him of things that he has read about but has never fully understood the import of, of the commingling of the dispassion of philosophy and the passion of faith. He learns of the fusion of the self and of a higher reality, the Brahman.

'We never claim that ours is the only or the true path,'

Rangababa insists. 'You choose it of your own volition. But if you choose this, you cannot stray.'

He has a question for Rangababa but something holds him back. He decides to save it for later.

He visits them once every year. Their attitude to him does not change much. He is an observer that they agree to tolerate and occasionally allow to dabble in their rites. On his third visit he finally asks Rangababa the question that he has saved for so long.

'Isn't killing another human being the ultimate taboo that society imposes? Isn't that the final barrier that I need to cross if I want to be truly free?'

The answer doesn't come as pat as they usually do. On his ash-smeared face his eyebrows are like little hillocks in a child's drawing that rise briefly as if in the midst of a quick tectonic shift. There is hardness in his stare as he slowly mulls over the answer. It comes slowly, carefully, well articulated, as if he is explaining the crux of the proof of a complex theorem.

'Our life on this earth is all maya, illusion. When Ishwar decides to trap us in this net of illusion and when he frees us is up to him. Who are we, mere mortals, to meddle in his plan?'

He is disappointed with the answer, feels that somehow things don't add up, that an internal logic of their philosophy has suddenly hit a wall of unreason. He does not persist, does not debate, but leaves quietly. He keeps visiting them for a couple of years after that but finds a change in Rangababa's attitude towards him. He knows that he has crossed a line somewhere and their tolerance towards him has thinned. He then stops visiting, knows that his learning there is over. He will not seek any more. It is up to him, the individual in isolation, to forge his own philosophy. A philosophy that does not encounter these sudden gaps of cogency but remains consistent and complete like a perfectly drawn circle.

# 30

# Randomness

Blue Cross hospital's gynaecology and obstetrics department is its cash cow and has a separate enclosure within the outpatients' wing. It has a forlorn look today with only a few patients perched on the bright orange bucket seats. The department's head and principal crowdpuller, Anita Sharma, is away for three days at a conference in the UK. The waiting area is bright and neon-light cheery with a muted television showing a news channel. There are stern warnings on the walls in both English and Bengali that prenatal sex determination is a crime that the hospital does not condone.

Arjun and Sohini walk up to the billing and registration counter, show their IDs and demand to see Usha Jain's files. Arjun had been to the hospital before when a colleague's son had an emergency appendectomy and knows that each patient is allotted a plastic folder containing the details of their treatment, their diagnostic reports, their stay at the hospital and copies of their bills. The clerk at the counter looks nervous as he walks into a small room that serves as the archive. The door is half open and the detectives see him pull out a file and flip through it.

Arjun can see the crease of a worry line on his forehead as he reads. He puts the file back, comes out and says he needs to speak to the head of administration. They wait.

The head, Rupali Ghosh Dastidar, is in her mid thirties, clad in an ill-fitting trouser suit. Her expression says that she is not willing to brook any nonsense.

'All the files are confidential. We cannot show you Usha's file unless you get a written approval from the director. He is in the UK with Dr Sharma.'

The quiet menace in Sohini's response reminds Arjun of Saikat Bhattacharya's interrogation over eight months ago. She looks Rupali in the eye and says, 'I presume you read the papers or at least watch television? Or do you just stick to the soaps? Anyway, we are the police and if you trust the news, the meanest bastards that you can find yourself dealing with. I am perfectly capable of arresting you now for illegal trade in organs. Or would you prefer fetal sex determination? Running a side trade in narcotics? Take your pick. We know how to plant the evidence.'

Rupali does not answer but her movements as she turns around, walks into the archive and fetches Usha Jain's file remind Arjun of a robot.

Buried under a pile of photocopies of prescriptions and diagnostic reports is a three-page summary of Usha Jain's many visits to the hospital. Sohini notices a pattern. The beginning of a pregnancy is clearly identifiable by an ultrasound test and a consultation with the gynaecologist. Its progression is marked by a second sonogram and a doctor's appointment early in the fourth month and soon after there is a brief mention of hospitalization for two days and then discharge. There are two such episodes.

What surprises her is that there are no details relating to these hospitalizations, no note on the cause for her stay. She rifles through the sheaf and is surprised to find nothing else on these periods, not even a simple blood test or a prescription for a painkiller.

She points to the sheets and asks Rupali for an explanation. Rupali is so terrified that it takes her a while to find her voice. 'Please believe me. I honestly have no idea. Dr Sharma is very…' she searches for a word, 'secretive about her files. She and the director will be back day after. The best I can do is to get hold of Dr Nahar. He occasionally helps Dr Sharma. I know he is in the wards at City Hospital now but I will make sure that he is here within an hour. You can wait. I'll get someone to open the VIP waiting room for you.'

Sohini says she will return in an hour. As they walk out, Arjun feels a gentle tap on his shoulder. He turns and sees a nurse, who hurriedly hands him a slip of paper, and then she is gone, a white blur walking through the swing doors at the end of the corridor.

The slip has her name, Pramila Sarkar, an address and a phone number. Usha Jain's name is written at the bottom.

—

This avenue was once the city's cinema strip. The Friday premieres had queues at the box office of over a kilometre long. If you were lucky, you could catch a glimpse of a favourite matinee idol, slick in his sharkskin suit or her georgette sari, oversized goggles and immaculately lacquered bouffant completing the ensemble. The scenes outside the theatres on Saturday evenings and the Sunday matinee seemed out of a riot. The street's decline began with the advent of video rentals, fun at home for half the price of a theatre ticket. Then the malls and their ubiquitous multiplexes came. That was the death knell. The ten cinema halls that flank both the sides of the avenue still stand. Three of them are boarded up and the rest converted into cramped shopping arcades and offices.

Pramila Sarkar lives in a tiny flat in a narrow by-lane behind one of the cinema halls. The two rooms and the tiny bathroom are clearly inadequate for its inhabitants – the nurse, her son who runs a small pest control business, a daughter afflicted by cerebral palsy and a nephew who goes to one of the city's colleges.

She claims to be fifty-two but she looks beaten, fatigued and at least ten years older.

'Money is tight,' she tells Arjun and Sohini as they sit on a bed that doubles as a couch during the day. 'I am talking to you because Lolita, my colleague, insisted and I genuinely cared for Usha. She helped me a lot. I want you to know the truth but I can't get caught up in your investigation. I need to work two shifts to put food on the table.'

Sohini pats her arm gently, assures her that she will ensure Pramila is not dragged into the case and the worst that can happen is that she will be asked to give witness in court. She still looks worried.

Sohini says, 'I promise to pick you up myself if you ever have to go to court and drop you back in a few hours. You have my word.'

'Well, you might have guessed by now that Usha was at the hospital for two abortions. Her babies were both girls. The hospital makes a pile from telling the parents if it's a boy or girl in the womb. They use both sonography and amniocentesis, where they shove a needle into the abdomen. A couple of years back, Dr Sharma went to the US to learn a new method that is less painful and detects the sex fairly early in the pregnancy. They offer this to some of the richer patients. But they are careful about who they deal with. They want references, and they cross-check everything. I don't know if you are aware that the director is Mrs Jain's cousin.

'I am just a contract employee at the hospital but Dr

Sharma trusts me. After Usha had her first abortion, she was in a real state. Didn't want to get out of bed or eat anything. The Jains wanted a full-time nurse and Dr Sharma recommended me. I forced her to eat, change her clothes, to start living again.'

Sohini lets her continue.

'This must have been about a year and a half ago. Then it was the same story all over again after a few months, the abortion followed by Usha's mental collapse. The Jains evidently trusted me and I stayed with her again for two months. They sent her to a mind doctor but I don't think it worked at all. Then she tried to kill herself about five months ago. The Jains wanted me back but I could only do the night shift. It was more like a guard's job than a nurse's, making sure that she didn't try to harm herself again. But things were better over the last few months; she told me that she was feeling happier, more positive. Then this terrible thing happened to her. Why her uncle chose to live in that godforsaken place beats me completely. Why did poor Usha have to go there?'

'Is there something else you want to tell us?' asks Arjun.

'Oh yes. She started scribbling in a notebook a few months ago. She always wrote at night. The Jains used to search her room regularly for anything that might incriminate them. So she gave it to me for safekeeping. I can't read a word of Hindi and I haven't shown it to anyone. Let me get it for you.'

She hands them a cheap notebook. Sohini flips through it. About fifteen pages of carefully written Devanagari script, wide spaces between the lines. She can make out from the first few pages that it is not a journal. It does not follow a chronological order or describe a day's events. She plans to read it on the way to her office.

Sohini and Arjun step out of Pramila's flat on to a sliver of pavement. She dials the number of Alpha Clinic she had taken from Hemant and asks to be put through to Dr Sen, the psychiatrist. Dr Sen is travelling and she is put through to his secretary. Sohini introduces herself, says she has questions about a patient.

'Are you asking about Usha Jain?' the secretary volunteers. She has heard of the murder. 'But she hasn't been Dr Sen's patient for a while. About five months back, Dr Sen handed her case over to the new doctor we have here. Sandip Chakraborty. There is a problem with our billing software. It still shows Usha as Dr Sen's patient. Dr Chakraborty will be in today. His clinic hours start from four. Do you want me to ask the appointments desk to block some time for you?'

'Thank you,' she says, 'that won't be necessary.'

That was the name she had been trying to recall when she was speaking to the Jains. Sandip Chakraborty was Ahona's psychiatrist.

The name triggers associations – the soothing smell of mouthwash, inflections of a southern accent with its unmistakable heaviness of the labial consonants, *My*

*Fair Lady* watched many times and degrees obtained at Pondicherry. MBBS in 1992.

Her mind works in strange ways. She cannot fathom why it takes this wholly unexpected twist, transporting her back to her undergraduate statistics classes almost three decades ago. All that fuss about probability and chance, of unbiased coins being tossed and unweighted, flawless dice being rolled, the probability distributions with their fancy European names – Gauss, Bernoulli, Poisson – man's attempts to find certainty in randomness, to second-guess god. She tries to frame a query in her head with the exactness of the questions that she remembers from her exam papers. What is the probability that a man who was privy to the deepest, most private thoughts of two women killed in exactly the same way was somehow...?

No, she is being silly. There are no unbiased coins in the real world, no unweighted dice. But her instinct tells her with a kind of absolute certainty that statisticians dislike that these two brutal killings are not random, unconnected acts. It tells her that the link between the two murders is Sandip Chakraborty.

# 31

# Revelations

The mid-morning traffic is heavy for some reason. Perhaps there's been an accident or a political rally that has started earlier than usual. The drive from Pramila's house to their office should have taken about half an hour but Sohini is reconciled to spending the next hour in the car. She asks Arjun to read aloud from the diary. He seems a little reticent, deterred by Ram Bahadur's presence. But Sohini assures him that the driver can be trusted – he has been with Sohini for over ten years.

Arjun reads in halting Hindi, his diction bearing the imprint of his mother tongue. He trips on words and has to repeat them. But Sohini is patient, she has her eyes shut and her ears seem to have grown used to the blaring horns outside, muffled partly by the rolled-up windows and the hum of the car's air conditioner.

The journal was clearly written at different points in time – there are breaks in the continuity, and the style and language show minor but discernible shifts.

*I am writing because he says that putting things down on paper will help ease the burden on my mind, I just hope no one reads this because if someone gets to know, I will die of shame.*

*I was so excited when I saw Hemant for the first time. I remember the baby pink shirt he wore and the Bangla sweets he had brought. Papa sold most of the shares he owned, his entire life's savings, on our wedding. The chandeliers looked so bright at our reception at Raigunj house that I thought they were made of Swarovski crystals.*

*When Hemant didn't even touch me on our wedding night, I thought he must be tired. Little did I know that Hemant would never touch me 'that way' ever, that he did not like women and the only person he wanted to touch was his best friend Ankit.*

*At first, Bauji and Mummy were so kind to me that I almost forgot the sadness I had felt on leaving home, of not being able to see Papa shaving in the morning or Ma watering the plants on our balcony.*

*Then things changed so suddenly. It began with a knock on the door on a night that Hemant was away in Ranchi. I opened the door and when I saw Bauji standing there, I was worried for him, thought he was ill and wanted me to call Dr Shome. I still couldn't understand what was happening when he bolted the door from inside and turned off the light.*

*God knows I struggled, bit him, pounded his back with my fists, raked it with my nails. But men are strong and after a few minutes the only thing I could do was give in. What saddened me the most was that while this was going on, Mummy was awake, perhaps even standing outside the bolted door. How could another woman, my own mother-in-law, let this happen to me?*

*When he left, there was a small red patch on the bed sheet. He had done to me what Hemant didn't or couldn't. I hid the sheet and threw it away later in that stinking garbage dump a few lanes away and turned the mattress over. I didn't want Keya, the maid who cleans the house and makes the bed, to suspect anything.*

*I have to confess that when I first felt a sign of life inside me I was happy. After all a child is a child. Does it really matter who the father is? Besides the blood that flows through her veins would be this family's blood, wouldn't it? There, I have given away the fact that I wanted a daughter. She would be stronger than me, make her own choices and not be trapped in the kind of web I am trapped in.*

*I had my suspicions on the day I went for my second ultrasound in my fourth month. I wondered why they had to put that long needle into my womb and draw that water out. It was like a really painful blood test although the doctor had earlier given me an injection to numb the pain. I am such a fool, always have been. I got to know much later this was amniocentesis, a way to find out if the unborn baby is a boy or girl.*

*We went back to the hospital a few days later. When the doctor asked me to leave the room and called them in, I knew they were up to something. Then they told me I was bearing a girl, that the fetus had a deformity and was unlikely to survive. I begged them to let me see the doctor, to show me the sonogram, point out where my womb had put such a deadly curse on the unborn child's body. But they didn't listen to me.*

*The week after the abortion, I could not move or even put a morsel in my mouth. I survived because of the milk and khichdi Pramila forced me to swallow. I wish I could be like her, accept the vagaries of fate so easily and not want to resist or fight.*

*Six months later the knocking on my door resumed and I realized that they were all working to a plan. Hemant would be away, Mummy would lock herself in her bedroom and then it would all start. I just wished all the hatred I now bore towards them would leave me barren. But god has strange plans and my womb was full again. There were no more lies this time. There were threats instead.*

*They wanted a male heir and if I didn't produce one, I would have to lose the child. If I kicked up a fuss, they would tell my family that the child was not Hemant's, that I had a lover who had fathered her. I know Papa loves me but the shock of this would kill him. I thought of going to the police but I knew that these people are capable of anything and the scandal that would follow would scathe only me and Papa but leave these people untouched. I gave in.*

*I know I have been foolish. I shouldn't have taken a blade to my wrist. But I felt so helpless then, thought I had nothing left in the world to live for. Papa knows but he has been silent about it even with me. Perhaps he wants to avoid a scandal or they have threatened him with something. I think my biggest mistake was to survive. After I came back from hospital, I became their prisoner. Thank god for Pramila. She is the only person who cares to talk to me.*

*Bauji hasn't touched me after I tried to end my life but I know it will start again soon. But I am stronger now with my new doctor at my side. I will resist, fight back and I know I will win this time. The old doctor just gave me pills that made me drowsy. This doctor gives me hope.*

*There is something about this man that makes me want to tell him all my secrets. There is magic in his eyes that seem to see into my soul. I like the way he listens to me without judging me, without fanning the hatred that I have in me. He knows about my suicide attempt but he has never chided me for it. He is the one person after Papa who really understands me. I can, and I do, tell him everything – from my heartbreaks and joys to my everyday routine.*

Arjun finishes reading. She had heard Arjun's voice crack with the strain of emotion as he read, but when she looks at him, she is surprised to see anger in this man she has always associated with a quiet equanimity. She sees it in his fists that are clenched tight, the quiver in his lips and the redness in his eyes where a thin film of tears has appeared despite his best efforts to suppress them. He nods his head in a jerky staccato up and down like a cheap doll with a spring neck, as if to compel himself to accept what he has read.

'We still have a long way to go,' she tells him quietly. 'Get a grip on yourself. Arjun, listen to me. We will throw the book at them – rape, abetment to suicide, gender selection – the works. But let's not get involved ourselves. Let the cops from the local station bring them in. We have to stick to our case.'

Every revelation yields a new possibility. Usha's scribbled notes make the Jain family suspect in her murder. Sohini is convinced that neither the son nor the father is capable of killing but wonders if they might have paid someone to do it for them. The crime branch has an entire dossier of hired killers and over the last few years junkies have flooded the market. Prices have dropped, kills going cheap, a life snuffed out for the price of some hits of smack.

But the notebook also endorses what her instinct tells her about the two murders. It makes the link in the chain stronger. Sohini lets her instinct guide her, to choose the path she will walk down. Sandip is now her prime suspect.

---

It takes them more than an hour to reach the crime branch. As they alight from the car, Sohini tells Arjun, 'Dr Chakraborty starts his clinic at four. I want you to get his home address, go there when he is away and see if you can find out where he was on the night of the murder.'

Arjun remembers the address from their meeting with the psychiatrist – Edward Court, an old colonial building close to the office district with ugly extensions done more recently, a hideous fusion of an old aesthetic and a young devil-may-care utilitarianism. While some of the old residents cling on to their ninety-nine-year leases, many other flats have been converted into guest houses or serviced apartments.

The guard, Swapan, is an amiable man in his fifties. He lives on the premises in a tiny room on the ground floor. He doesn't seem particularly intimidated when Arjun flashes his police ID and is more than willing to talk.

'Yes, I know Doctorbabu well. No, he wasn't here on the night you mention and hasn't been in Edward Court for the last few days. But that's not unusual for him. He is a lonely man, never has visitors. He occasionally spends a few days at his uncle's place. I never quite asked where his uncle lives.

But hold on, he might be at that medical camp somewhere in the outskirts of the city. He went there about a week ago just for a day. Made a royal mess of his car. It was covered in dirty red mud. He took it to a garage immediately; otherwise the muck would have dried completely. When he left again with a small suitcase on Wednesday, I assumed he was going back to the camp.'

Wednesday was the day of Usha Jain's murder. Sandip must have gone to Lalmati a week ago to do a…the English word eludes Arjun though he knows it begins with 'r'…yes, 'reconnaissance', that's it. That's when the tawny red mud of Lalmati had clung to his car. Then he went back on the day of the killing. Usha Jain must have mentioned her visit to her aunt's place possibly during her last therapy session. He calls Sohini.

# 32

# Shantidham

Ram Bahadur is a little surprised when they drive all the way down to Alpha Clinic but Sohini doesn't go in. She asks him to park a few hundred yards away from the entrance and they wait. They can see the main entrance of the clinic from here. It is almost seven but they have to wait a good half hour before the throng of patients thins and Sandip finally emerges, clad in a well-cut suit. He disappears into the parking lot and emerges after a few minutes at the wheel of a black Honda City. They wait for a minute and follow.

He does not go in the direction of Edward Court but instead drives west, towards the river. The traffic is still sluggish and they have been on his tail for almost an hour when Sandip's car turns into a lane off the main road that connects the city's south-west to its centre. This lane leads to an old neighbourhood once favoured by colonial officials and expatriate company bosses for its proximity to the river and the cool breeze that blows across the water at the end of hot summer days. Most of the large breezy bungalows have been torn down to make way for high-rise apartment blocks.

As he drives further down, the apartment blocks give way to construction sites, buildings being torn down or foundations being excavated. Finally the car stops at the entrance of a house that the builders seem to have left alone. Sandip opens the large rusty iron gates and drives in. Sohini waits for a while, gets down from her car and walks to the gate. It is dark but she can make out a large, unkempt garden, the grass so tall that it seems like a field of wheat.

Sandip has disappeared into the dark, unlit house at the end of the driveway. It is a large three-storeyed house, but from what she can make out in the dark, it is in ruins. After about ten minutes, she sees a light come on in the top floor.

The pillars that flank the gate have marble plaques. The black lettering has faded a little but when she shines her torch on the plaque on the right she can make out the name Dr Amaresh Bakshi with the well-known acronyms MBBS, FRCP below it. The plaque on the left says 'Shantidham', abode of peace, and below it is a name printed with excessive serif, Harihar Bakshi.

She waits for an hour. Sandip does not emerge and she drives away.

---

She knows what to do next – find out about Amaresh Bakshi and Harihar Bakshi. She scrolls down her phone's address book and dials a number.

Dr Sushobhan Bagchi is in his seventies. He has retired but only technically in that he does not have a salaried position at a hospital. He sees patients at home and there is always a throng of patients waiting to consult this legendary endocrinologist. Bagchi's reputation as a doctor is matched by his reputation as a gossip and a repository of information about the city's medical community. He has become a little rusty of late; he hasn't kept pace with the invasion of new doctors with their fancy clothes and penchant for invasive medical tests.

But he is still the gold standard when it comes to his peers – knows every lapse, misdeed and peccadillo of theirs. Sohini had consulted him years ago on a couple of cases involving a leading surgeon of the city and an anaesthetist. She remembers that he does not expect anything in return for his assistance, just a patient listener for his endless fund of stories. She still can't decide whether she likes this genial man or loathes his unabashed and obsessive curiosity about other people's lives.

'I am surprised you haven't heard of Amaresh Bakshi,' he tells her. 'The man was a legend. Finest cardiologist the city's ever had. Pity his personal life was such a shambles. Wife topped herself. The rumour was that she was sleeping with a cousin of sorts and Amaresh found them in flagrante delicto. His father was a businessman, a construction czar. Can't recall his name. Amaresh left the city after his father died. Became the principal of the new institute for heart sciences in Madras. His son was in his early teens then. Unfortunately the boy had a spot of trouble – he was expelled from the Madras Medical College.'

'Are you sure that his son studied in Madras and not Pondicherry?'

'Sohini, you know I don't make these mistakes and despite my age my memory isn't getting weaker. Must be all the fish I eat. Amaresh and his son were both in Madras. Incidentally, I have a friend who taught at the medical college at that time. He is likely to know exactly what the son had done. T.R.S. Subramaniam. He is of course retired now but I know he lives somewhere in Madras. Reticent chap though, unlike me. Even if you can get his number, I doubt he will say much on the phone. I can also check if my friend Balaji can help you. I was a visiting consultant at his hospital for years. Got to know him well. He was a student at the Madras Medical College. He's about the same age as Bakshi's son if I'm right. Might have even been his classmate. I will text his number to you.'

'Thank you very much, sir. I owe you dinner at least. Let me know when you are free and pick a restaurant.'

'Always a pleasure. I'm not going to say no to dinner, though. Incidentally, the grapevine tells me you are drinking like a fish. You have to watch yourself, Sohini. You are at a difficult age.'

# 33

# Decisions

How he hates this life of constant flight, twigs gathered, nests built and then the inevitable sense of danger and he has to fly again. He knows that he must hurry. Unlike his previous flights, this is not a matter of precaution, indulgence of his overcareful nature. It is now an imperative, a stark choice between freedom and incarceration and most likely death.

Dr Sen's secretary has told him of that woman's telephone call. The white car in his rear-view mirror last evening doggedly on his trail must have been hers. What bothers him the most is that she has not called him afterwards or met him at the clinic. He fears that his next encounter with her will be a knock on his door at an unexpected moment, a warrant flourished and cocked guns pointed at his forehead.

But something is holding him back. He is weary to

the bone, tired of the constant running, of the lies, the dissembling, of the identities that he needs to don, the stories behind these identities that he has to fabricate. He wants this fugitive life to end even if it means a tightly knotted hemp rope around his neck, the rough fibres strafing the delicate skin and then the swing of the trapdoor as his body plunges in, the vertebrae snapping one after another khut, khut, khut.

Before that he wants his last moments of transcendence, the feel of a woman's hair in the vice-like grip of his left fist, his right fist around the smooth wooden handle of the cleaver aloft and the sweeping arc of its descent. He has chosen his victim.

The last few days of his manic research have given him a glimpse into the life of the middle-aged police officer who is now his pursuer. He wishes he had just that one chance to talk to her across a table, patient to doctor, but knows that it is not possible. Yet the news clips that he has pored over on the Internet have given him a sense of her life, the roller-coaster swings of her career and the inevitable turmoil that must have wreaked.

He has read that she is single and he imagines her as lonely, friendless, her nights suffused with the agony of solitariness. He will release her from this barrenness and turmoil, offer her his final benediction.

'You are asking for too many things,' Anish Lall says. 'Don't get me wrong. I am not disputing what you or Mr Maity are saying. I am not dismissing your hypothesis altogether. We could well be dealing with a serial killer but I am against reopening the Chatterjee case with the little evidence you have. I can agree to your bringing the doctor in for questioning in the Lalmati case but again let me be honest – what you have on him is circumstantial and that too if I stretch the definition of the word.'

Sohini, DCM, Arjun and Anish are seated on the sofa in the commissioner's room. There is a pile of crime scene photographs and reports on the long glass-top coffee table. These photos are from both murders, Ahona's and Usha's, as are the post-mortem reports. Usha's autopsy was done at the Lalmati hospital by a junior general surgeon. The hospital forensic unit was shut down a few years ago, victim of a fiscal crunch in the state. DCM is clearly not happy with the quality of the report although it does corroborate the fact that the murder weapon was a relatively straight blade, not a sickle. The injury to the head was superficial and possibly made, the surgeon has noted, with a blunt instrument. There is no visible trauma to the brain but the blow could have caused mild concussion. The wound to the neck is identical to Ahona's. The blade severed the spinal cord, the internal jugulars and the carotid arteries before coming to rest just short of the neck muscles. There is a brief mention of the scar on her left wrist.

The crime scene forensic report also rests on the coffee

table between the blue plastic covers of a folder. Joyonto Bose, the young investigator, seems to have done a thorough job and the garrulous Shyamal Ghosh has ensured that the crime scene remained somewhat pristine, unlike Ahona's flat. The only fingerprints found at the site are Usha's and of the three policemen at the scene. There are footmarks but no footprints.

Anish Lall worries for Sohini, worries that she is again headed down a path that is a dead end. He has always liked this frail woman, a misfit or so he believes in this world of deceit and corruption. He knows her brittleness, her tendency to turn on herself with booze, pills and god knows what when she faces disappointment. He knows that this is her last shot at personal and professional redemption. She will not survive another defeat.

'Sir,' she says, 'I am worried that the suspect will run. We have just two constables outside Shantidham. They tell me he is holed up there and the clinic says he hasn't been in for the last four days. But you can never tell with these things. We need a couple of more people guarding the house. Arjun's got hold of a recent photograph of his from the clinic. It was used to make his identity card at the clinic. Can we circulate it among the security people at the airports, bus terminals and railway stations?'

Anish agrees.

'Sir, I want to go to Chennai. If I can find out what happened there and if indeed Sandip is Dr Bakshi's son, we'll have a better case to take him into custody.'

# 34

# Chennai

Sohini flies that afternoon in one of the cut-price airlines in a middle seat with so little leg room that her knees keep knocking on the seat in front. Her neighbour in the window seat is a heavy sleeper, a snorer with sleep apnoea so that he wakes up at intervals, red-eyed and startled, surprised to find himself where he is and then goes back to his slumber.

A baby two seats away wails throughout the flight as his sad-eyed mother, bone-tired from the weariness of early motherhood, tries to pacify him for a while and then gives up.

The sandwich Sohini buys is cardboard dry but comes in a pretty box. She pops two pills to buy herself an hour of chemical tranquillity. She will sleep them off later in her hotel.

She arrives in Chennai at six-thirty in the evening and as she alights the slight but distinct briny stench of the sea greets her. She hires a taxi to her hotel, government approved, which wipes out her measly daily allowance. She is afraid of the inevitable bed bugs, sheets with maplike stains of old dried semen and stinky loos.

She keeps telling herself that it is only for a night as she goes down the main arterial road of the city. The rush hour traffic is heavy and her taxi crawls. She gapes at the skyscraper-sized posters, the actors with lurid pink skin, and the queues at the arrack shops and dozes off.

She wakes up with a start, the hotel is still a few kilometres away and she rings the two doctors whose numbers she has got from Dr Bagchi. They have been expecting her call and agree to meet her the next morning.

Her first meeting is with Balaji, a neurologist with one of the large hospitals that flaunts an American collaboration. Balaji got his MBBS degree in 1992, the same year that Sandip claims to have graduated. However, he doesn't remember him.

'It was a large class,' he says, 'impossible to remember everyone. But I do remember a Bengali guy from the 1993 batch. He was in the first year but then there was some kind of scandal. None of us got to know what it was really about. We all thought he had tried to molest one of the night-duty nurses. He was expelled overnight. I remember his father was a hotshot doctor. He was the principal of the Advanced Institute for Cardiac Sciences. Also a member of the national council of the Indian Medical Association.'

'Would you recognize him if I showed you his photograph?' Sohini asks.

'It's unlikely. I am terrible at remembering faces and it's been almost thirty years. But hold on. Shiva from our class is very active in our alumni association. He recently posted some group photographs and there's one of all of the 1993 class at the beginning of the first year. Here, let me show you the photographs on our Facebook alumni page. Let's see if you can recognize him.'

There are four photographs posted by Shiva followed by a long string of comments.

The photograph of the new inductees is a little grainy but scanned well. Second from the left on the third row of fresh-faced graduates is a scrawny boy with wild hair and a wisp of a moustache. His extreme fairness, highlighted in monochrome, gives him away. Sohini is sure that this is Sandip Chakraborty twenty-five years ago but the legend that identifies him at the bottom of the photograph says Sudipto Bakshi.

---

T.R.S. Subramaniam retired from the medical college twelve years ago. He is a pathologist but has kept in touch with the college, attends some of the conferences and delivers the occasional guest lecture. He lives in a small, white, single-storeyed house just off East Coast Road.

Sohini and TRS sit in the small but neat garden as Rajan, the household help, fetches them coffee. TRS's wife is a moderately successful classical singer, a disciple of the great M.S. Subbulakshmi. She is teaching a class in the living room; the student seems adept and Sohini finds the choral strains of Raag Hindolam soothing.

TRS is reluctant to talk.

'All that happened so long ago. Why do you want to rake up the past?' he asks.

'Sir, this might help solve a case involving multiple murders,' Sohini says.

---

It's been a tiring day for TRS. Three lectures in the morning followed by the monthly inspection of the hostel rooms. By the time he finishes it is eight-thirty in the evening. He has two lectures the next day but mercifully they are both in the afternoon. He wishes he hadn't taken on freelance forensic work from the police but the woman's body is lying in the autopsy room. It's a young woman and there are no external injuries. He knows what he will find – internal trauma to the brain and traces of the seepage of blood in other recesses of the body where there was impact. He decides to go to his room, have dinner and catch a few hours of sleep before he returns and starts working on the cadaver.

When he sets off for the autopsy room it's three in the

morning. He is surprised to find the light on and when he enters the blast of the air conditioner hits him. He can see the new Bengali student standing next to the cadaver that has been turned over and is lying on its belly. The instrument he is holding is not surgical; it seems like a large meat cleaver. He notices that he has attempted to decapitate the cadaver. He has been partly successful but hasn't been able to cut through the neck entirely.

The boy seems to be in a trance, the cleaver hanging loosely from his right hand. He does not register TRS's presence. TRS feels a slow numbing of limbs and then his mind as if his entire being wants to shut out this gruesome vision. He regains his composure, locks the door from outside and rushes off to the small office next to the autopsy room. He knows the boy's father, knows that his institute has an emergency line since it is also a large hospital. He calls and gets Amaresh Bakshi's home number.

From the time Dr Bakshi arrives to when they leave together the father and son do not exchange a single word. The vice principal is summoned, the boy is to be expelled immediately, an accusation of sexual assault is fabricated and TRS spends the next hour attaching the severed head back to the body with a needle and surgical thread. He hopes the police will buy his explanation that this was essential to the autopsy.

---

'I was so devastated I could barely eat or sleep for the next few days. I can still describe in vivid detail what I saw that night as I opened the door to the autopsy room. What saved me was my faith in my god and I have been closer to him since.'

---

Sohini's flight leaves at six. She has been on a long conference call with her colleagues and Subhendubabu has been patched in. There's been a development. A judge signed the papers for taking Sandip into judicial custody and Lall had sent three constables to Shantidham in the afternoon to bring him in. But as they entered the compound and approached the house, gunshots rang out. They were fired from the third floor but either the shooter's aim was poor or they were meant just to intimidate the intruders, not to wound or maim.

The police now have a reason to arrest Sandip. He is in their parlance 'armed and dangerous' and resisting custody. They will raid the house in the morning and Sohini wants to lead the raid team. Anish decides to indulge her but insists that the raiding posse carry guns and wear bulletproof jackets. Sohini hates the idea of wearing this heavy, pore-less armour in the sweltering heat and tries to bargain with Lall. But he is adamant and Sohini gives in.

# 35

# Affection

**Thirty-four years ago**

Harihar lies on his side on an ornate bed made of dark, varnished Burma teak. There are elaborate designs on the headboard with a centrepiece that shows two peacocks facing each other as if poised to fight over a mate. The four supports that the bed rests on are like a lion's claws. This eclectic design does not have a unifying theme. The carpenter appears to have got carried away and the effect is that of a fantastic beast without identifiable mythological provenance.

Harihar is seventy-six and in the past five years has been felled by two cerebral strokes that have paralysed most of his body. There is drool hanging in a delicate balance from the left side of his mouth like gossamer. He has wet himself again. He whispers something repetitively. Bhola, his manservant, knows this single word uttered like an incantation is the term of endearment reserved only for grandsons, 'Dadubhai'.

Despite his incapacitation, a part of his mind is still alive. He recognizes the song playing on the Murphy gramophone placed next to the bed. It is Gyan Gosain singing 'Nat Malhar'. This is a particular favourite of his. It portrays the young Krishna dancing and there are two lines that bring an invisible smile to his lips.

*Chorone noopur baje*
*Roonu jhoonu taal*
(As he dances, his anklets beat a tinkling rhythm – roonu jhoonu, roonu jhoonu)

It brings back memories of his grandson, Boobun, as a two-year-old trying to dance to this song with a baby's endearing clumsiness as he, Harihar, clapped a rhythm. He knows that Boobun, now fourteen, is standing outside his room, watching him with his intense stare. He stopped coming in after his second stroke three years ago. He wishes there was a way in which he could reach out to this motherless adolescent, find a way to make him overcome the revulsion he feels towards his invalid grandfather.

He feels a pang of self-pity for what he, once the construction czar of this state, the man who was responsible for building a quarter of the state's arterial roads and bridges, has been reduced to. He did not come from old money. To use his favourite English phrase, he is 'self-made'.

Nabogopal, a vegetable wholesaler's assistant, had invested a small sum in iron ingots at the start of the First World War on the advice of his employer, Kalindi Ghosh. Ghosh's only addiction apart from the snuff he frequently snorted was international politics and he read every newspaper that he could lay his hands on.

*'Nabo, tui loha ken,'* was his terse tip to his young assistant – to buy iron – as he counted cauliflowers in his godown. The investment based on this tip quadrupled by the end of the war. Nabogopal, the archetype of the lower-middle-class Bengali salaried man, had cashed out his investment and deposited the sum in a bank. The miracle of compound interest meant that two decades later when Harihar, barely out of his teens, had showed an inclination towards business, his father had been able to hand him enough to start a small 'contracting' business. This by the sixties grew into the construction giant whose only serious business rival was Dubash Industries.

Harihar often muses on the few regrets that he had in his life – his decision not to consult a senior obstetrician despite his wife's prenatal complications, thus leaving her to die in the hands of his friend Mukul just out of medical college; his inability to convince his son Amaresh to join the family business instead of pursuing medicine; his reluctance to intervene when the rows between Amaresh and his wife became increasingly vicious, finally prompting her to take her own life. What he regrets the most is his body's refusal to enable him to take care of his only grandchild. He still shudders to think that the small child was the first to discover his mother's body, to find her hanging from the hook of the ceiling fan as he walked in to look for his school socks.

Bhola is the only one in the household who believes that his master of the last forty years can still hear and understand. He keeps chattering as he bathes him, wipes his shit, showers him with talcum and changes his clothes. He tells him that the boy has no friends and locks himself away in a corner room on the first floor whenever at home. At times he has seen the boy in a trance, as if possessed by a spirit.

These regrets and the lacquer records that Bhola plays for him through the day and half the night give him a will to live. He still wants to make amends and reverse the irreversible.

—

Boobun has waited three long years for this, prepared his mind and body to carry out this act. Much that he has exercised his body, repeated push-ups till he collapsed in an exhausted heap, lifted the two bricks lying on the terrace till the spasms in his upper arm muscles ran atremble through his entire body, he knows that he is not strong enough to build sufficient force in a cleaver's momentum to sever a human head from the body. He practises on the kittens that the stray cat that sheltered herself in the corner of the veranda had birthed. He uses the small kitchen cleaver that the cook Romen uses to chop the large cuts of mutton into small curry-sized pieces and then buries the bodies and heads carefully in the vacant plot next to their house.

Deep within him is an awareness, an understanding that taking a human life is as much about the strength of the mind as it is of the body, the sheer will to look into the terrified eyes of the victim and not be overcome by guilt or pity. He knows he needs a different kind of practice, a rehearsal of his mind's performance.

When he considers a possible quarry to help in his rehearsal he thinks of the inert old man lying upstairs in his piss-soaked pyjamas on a piss-soaked bed. His life now, he knows, is a waste. All those medicines being injected into him morning and evening just to make him breathe and mess himself so badly are but the vanity of wealth, of the ability to secure the means of staying alive when there is really no reason to live.

---

Bhola is sleeping on the floor on a thin mattress, snoring and occasionally murmuring in his sleep. The night is unusually still and the windows have been left open in the hope of a stray breeze. There is a streak of dim mercury luminescence falling on the side of the bed where the old man is sleeping and before he approaches him he picks up a pillow from the other side of the bed.

As he stands next to his grandfather, he can see by the dirty white light from the street lamp that his eyes are wide open. As he brings the pillow down to his face, he does not see terror but bafflement. The old man's lips move and he can hear an almost silent whisper, *'Keno? Keno?'* Why? Why?

As he presses the pillow down on his face, his mind is suddenly flooded with memories. They take him back to a winter afternoon at Shoriker Dhal, of weak sunshine, of his grandfather bowling to him with a tennis ball and Bhola crouching behind him in a copybook wicketkeeper's pose. He remembers the heaviness of the lacquer records and the thrill he felt when he was allowed to slide the records through the spoke of the gramophone, of holding his grandfather's hand tight as he watched them take his mother's body away, of begging him never, never to leave him.

He throws the pillow away, makes sure that Harihar is still breathing and tiptoes out of the room. The rehearsal is over. He has flubbed his lines.

Two days later, Harihar dies of his third cerebral stroke.

# 36

# The Raid

This is how the monsoon begins. A week of unrelenting heat with the vertical near-equinox sun's rays beating down tirelessly. And then this dark morning, the sky thick with a mass of dark nimbus clouds, static electricity in the air spiking up the hair on the head and forearms, all portending a thunderstorm. It is dark even though it is just eleven in the morning. The cloud cover traps the heat and there is a sweltering, disturbed broodiness in the air that will soon erupt in a rage.

Arjun hates this kind of weather. It takes him back to his childhood, his acute fear of thunder and lightning, sheltering under his father's bed with early summer nor'westers pounding the city. He has overcome this through years of determination, will power and self-suggestion. He has read somewhere that this is a primal fear, an alarm system to alert the human mind against danger that evolution has ironed out in most humans. Thus he is an unlucky freak, a flaw in the grand march of human progress whose brain remains hardwired, unable to turn the alarm off, ever fearful that at some unexpected moment it will start ringing again.

Indeed, it has surfaced in the past in moments of crisis or deep anxiety and the two fears have mingled, feeding off each other in an unbridled symbiosis, getting fatter, filling his brain and then taking hold of his entire body.

—

Four of them enter the portico of Shantidham and climb up three marble steps that lead to the main door. Two constables follow Sohini and Arjun. All of them are wearing heavy green bulletproof jackets, made of synthetic fabric, that makes them sweat profusely. These are borrowed from the anti-terrorism unit of the city police. They are oversized, and their sheer heft crimps their movement, forcing them to shrug one shoulder after the other like marionettes to feel more comfortable.

Sohini suddenly remembers the flurry of newspaper articles alleging massive kickbacks in their bulk purchase by the government just a couple of years ago. She also remembers the ballistics experts' interviews during that time who had questioned the efficacy of these jackets against real bullets, the cheap Chinese knock-off synthetic used in them not a patch on the Kevlar that goes into the better versions.

They turn the brass handle green with patina and find it open. As they push the heavy wooden door a gush of trapped, fetid air assails them. It is dark inside, the wooden windows are shuttered and there is a nauseating smell of animal or bird shit. They shine their torches and see they are in a large living room full of mismatched bits of furniture like an auctioneer's warehouse covered in layers of dust. At the end of the room there are two flights of curved stairs on either side of the back wall, straight out of an old film set, that lead to the floor above.

Sohini asks them to take their revolvers out and gingerly takes out her own Smith and Wesson 0.38, a hand-me-down from the army, that was tucked into her belt at the back. Arjun has a Ruger Service Six and the constables have FIE Titan Tigers, standard service revolvers of the police force. The torches are mercifully small and they hold them between their teeth as they unlock the safety catches and hold their revolvers in both hands.

Sohini's hands tremble as she holds hers. She is completely out of practice, having consistently dodged her mandatory firing schedule ever since she moved to civil defence. However, holding a torch between the teeth is no mean feat, the nerves in their front teeth tingle and they follow a curious pantomime of taking one hand off the revolver, holding the torch for a few seconds and then it's both hands on the gun, torch between their teeth again.

The steps are wooden, the rotting wood covered with coir matting. The first casualty of their raid happens as constable Shanti Ghatak's foot goes straight through a step that has decayed completely. He screams and from the distinct crack Arjun hears he knows he has broken a bone. Sohini instructs the other constable, Rajkumar Singh, to assist him. Singh struggles out of his bulletproof jacket and sits gingerly on the steps next to his colleague.

The first floor is equally dark but by the light of their torches they can make out a long corridor with rooms on either side. There is a curious rustling sound and they look up to find an army of bats hanging from the exposed rafters flapping their wings in protest against the sudden intrusion of light. Sohini calls out, 'Sudiptobabu, Sudipto Bakshi, are you there? Please come out with your arms raised. We are the police.'

There is no answer but a sudden shard of light illuminates the corridor and is followed by a loud rumble of thunder. Sohini wonders where the light came from and realizes there is a glass window at the end of the corridor blocked by a large wooden cupboard.

Arjun freezes. The boy in him who hid under the bed, eyes shut, fingers plugging his ears and counting to a hundred, a thousand, a million until the storm dissipated is suddenly back. He wants to throw away the revolver, shield his eyes, cover his ears and crouch under the stairs... Sohini notices that something is amiss, that he is afraid, and tells him,

'Arjun, you can't afford to lose your nerve now. It's just the two of us.'

They go down the corridor, Sohini leading and Arjun, chastised, following mechanically with his gun raised, his mind alert only to the next roll of thunder. They find a stairway leading to the top floor of the house. As they climb, they see a weak light on the steps perhaps from an open window upstairs. The staleness of the air has diminished and they get the smell of wet earth that has wafted up from the garden below. There are also signs of repair – the steps are sturdier and the wall on their side seems to have had a recent coat of paint.

It gets brighter as they get to the next floor and finally they find themselves in a long, closed balcony. The tall wooden windows are shuttered except for one at the far end that is open. Through it they can see a mass of green leaves and a sliver of the sky, still grey and angry. The furniture in the room is antique but polished and in good condition and the chessboard floor of black and white marble seems clean.

Arjun thinks that the storm is ending but then there is a sudden blinding glow of sheet lightning that sprints across the sky; he shuts his eyes in an involuntary reflex and the thunder comes with a quick low hiss, an ear-splitting crack and then an evanescent roll.

Arjun forces himself to open his eyes and finds Sudipto facing him. He stands between Arjun and Sohini, who continues to inch her way forward unaware. What catches

Arjun's attention immediately is the fairness of Sudipto's hairless torso, so fair in this weak light that it seems to have a luminescence of its own. As his eyes travel down to the dense mass of his pubes, of his slightly tumescent penis, he feels the blow on his skull. Arjun crumples to the floor, feeling the warm ooze of blood slowly spreading over his scalp, and he blacks out.

He does not know how many minutes or hours have passed when he regains consciousness and at first all he sees is a blur. As his eyes regain focus, his entire body shudders at the sight before him, sending a sharp spasm of pain through his skull. Sohini is kneeling on the floor about ten feet away from him. There is a streak of blood running from her hair down to her right cheek, stopping suddenly there like a river dammed. He guesses she too has been hit on the head. Her hands seem tied behind her back.

Sudipto is behind her, his left hand trying to get a firmer purchase on her short hair. He holds a raised cleaver in his right hand preparing to strike and has the intense concentration of a craftsman putting the final touches to his creation. What he cannot fathom though is the expression on Sohini's face. It is surprisingly serene without a trace of fear. She is either concussed or has made peace with her impending death. Her beheading.

Arjun's gun is on the floor about four feet away; he knows the safety catch is off. But his strength seems to have ebbed with the blow to his head, the pain has numbed his faculties.

For a moment he feels like giving in to the throbbing ache, to get some moments of rest. Words float in and out of his mind. They seem neatly wrapped like thought bubbles in a comic book – 'bravery', 'courage' – and his mind clutches at them to fend off his inertia. He heaves himself up and crawls on all fours like a baby towards the gun when Sudipto notices him.

Sudipto lets go of Sohini, who slumps to the floor, kicks her in the face and strides towards Arjun in giant leaps like a moonwalker. When he raises his cleaver to strike, Arjun has his trembling fingers around the trigger. He is balancing on one elbow and his knees, too disoriented to aim, but he shoots so that the explosion distracts Sudipto. He hears the sound of the bullet hitting flesh, sees the burn-hole in his stomach, near the solar plexus, the manipur chakra, and then the blood starts pouring out.

He blacks out again and when he opens his eyes there is an entire posse of policemen entering the balcony, revolvers cocked, shouting 'Put your hands in the air!' To him they don't matter, they are actors in another play that by happenstance is being enacted on the same stage. He seems to find strength for just one more thing. He calls out, 'Madam? Madam?'

He hears her groan as if to answer his question, to confirm that she is conscious. Arjun is now at peace; he lets the pain overcome him and he closes his eyes.

# Epilogue

Sohini opens her eyes to find herself in a hospital bed with a muted television in front of her. She can feel the heavy bandage on her head, a slight numbness in her face and the slight tingle in her hand where a drip is inserted. She hears the beep of a monitor. Sajal is sitting next to her, looking anxious, and her mother is near the door talking to a nurse. Her first question is about Arjun.

'He is recovering well. He was in the ICU for a while but they've taken him out. He is in the next ward,' Sajal replies. 'How are you feeling? How is the pain? You have been sedated for more than a day now.'

Bani rushes to her bedside and holds her hand. The commissioner, DCM and even Subhendubabu have visited. Sohini can't suppress a smile when she sees Archishman Basu's card hanging from a gigantic bouquet of carnations next to her bed.

She wants to talk more, know what happened after she passed out on the marble floor, but Bani insists that she needs what the doctor has described as 'complete' rest. That evidently means she should not talk much or at least about things that could cause stress or excitement. Bani tells her the stricture of complete rest holds for at least four days.

---

The nurse on duty in Arjun's room wonders if she should fetch the doctor. Her patient, still heavily sedated, seems agitated, tossing and turning under the thick green blanket, and his eyelids keep flickering rapidly. She then realizes that he is having a nightmare and walks towards the bed.

Arjun dreams that he is on a long, narrow boat in the middle of a muddy river. The boatman looks familiar and though he can't quite make out his face, the pale, bare torso tells him that it is Sudipto. There is a woman sitting on a slat in the middle and, though her back is turned to him, he guesses from her short, cropped hair and ill-fitting shirt that it is Sohini. In a matter of seconds, the boatman's oar morphs into a cleaver which he raises as he walks towards her on the swaying boat. He notices that she has a gun in her hand pointed at the boatman but seems unable to shoot. Arjun is petrified and starts screaming, '*Gooli korun, madam, gooli korun.*' (Shoot, madam, shoot.) He then feels a cool hand on his shoulder, a strong smell of sanitizer and a voice from the distance, 'Wake up, Arjunbabu, you're having a bad dream.'

---

There is always a sense of incompleteness, a lack of closure in murder cases involving a psychopath, even when he is apprehended and a decisive end put to his trail of butchery. Most cops believe that this stems from the fact that the holy grail of an investigation, the motive for the crime, is absent or so deeply hidden in the recesses of a deranged mind that it is impossible to find.

The crime branch now has reams of information on Harihar Bakshi, Amaresh Bakshi and his wife Mandira who committed suicide at the age of thirty-two. The police files have attributed the suicide to deep depression. Amaresh is alive but in an advanced state of Alzheimer's disease, languishing in a tiny flat in Pondicherry in the care of an ageing servant.

Bhola is dead; the other retainers of Shantidham and members of the Bakshi family are dead or untraceable. A maid who came to the house twice a week to clean and swab has been questioned but her only contact with Sudipto was one day at the end of the month when she got paid. She has never seen the ground or first floor of the house and used the iron spiral staircase at the back of the house that provided an entry through the bathroom.

His fake degrees from Pondicherry have been discovered and a forensic expert has pointed to a glaring flaw in the forgery of the registrar's signature.

This veritable wall of information is in the public domain, in the thousands of column inches that newspapers have devoted to the case and in carefully transcribed police files. But there are gaping holes in this wall. Sohini, her colleagues or the many journalists who are sifting and will sift through this mound of data will never know of that moonless evening in Shoriker Dhal, the pillow pressing down on Harihar's face as he struggled for breath or Rangababa's eyebrows rising on his ash-smeared face. They will never know of the twisted philosophy of a motherless young man's search for transcendence.

---

Sohini's eyes turn to the television screen, the sound still muted. A familiar news channel is reporting on the decomposed body of a teenage girl evidently from one of the city's best schools found in the horticultural gardens, yet another legacy of the city's colonial past. There are pixelated images of the girl's body partly concealed by a clump of bushes and shots of the distraught parents. Sohini hopes she will be assigned the case.

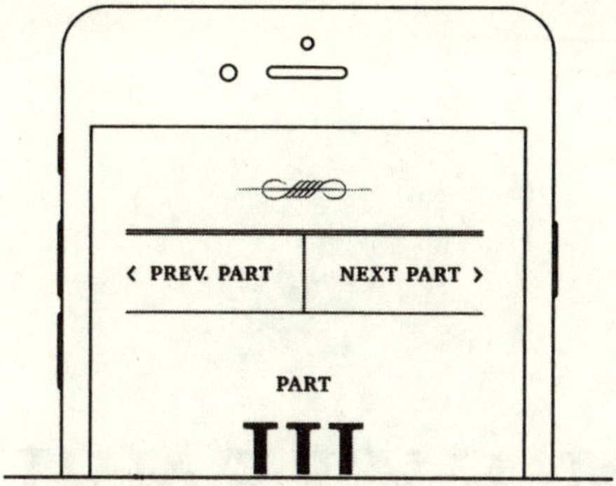


## Beautiful Typography

The quality of print transferred to your mobile. Forget ugly PDFs.

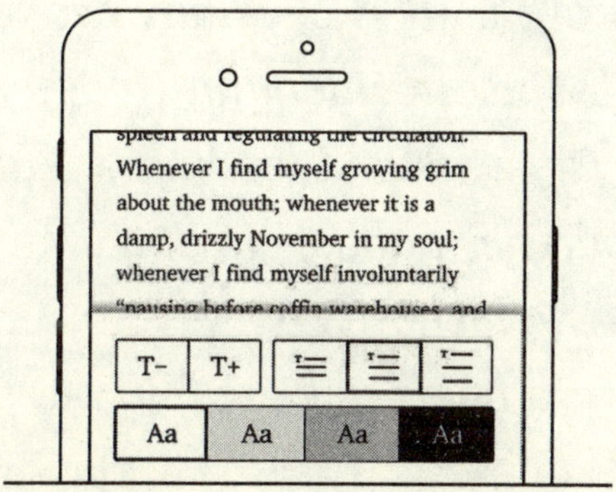


## Customizable Reading

Read in the font size, spacing and background of your liking.

# AN EXTENSIVE LIBRARY

*Including fresh, new, original Juggernaut books from the likes of Sunny Leone, Praveen Swami, Husain Haqqani, Umera Ahmed, Rujuta Diwekar and lots more. Plus, books from partner publishers and loads of free classics. Whichever genre you like, there's a book waiting for you.*

juggernaut.in

# DON'T JUST READ; INTERACT

*We're changing the reading experience from passive to active.*

## Ask authors questions

Get all your answers from the horse's mouth. Juggernaut authors actually reply to every question they can.

## Rate and review

Let everyone know of your favourite reads or critique the finer points of a book – you will be heard in a community of like-minded readers.

## Gift books to friends

For a book-lover, there's no nicer gift than a book personally picked. You can even do it anonymously if you like.

## Enjoy new book formats

Discover serials released in parts over time, picture books including comics, and story-bundles at discounted rates. And coming soon, audiobooks.

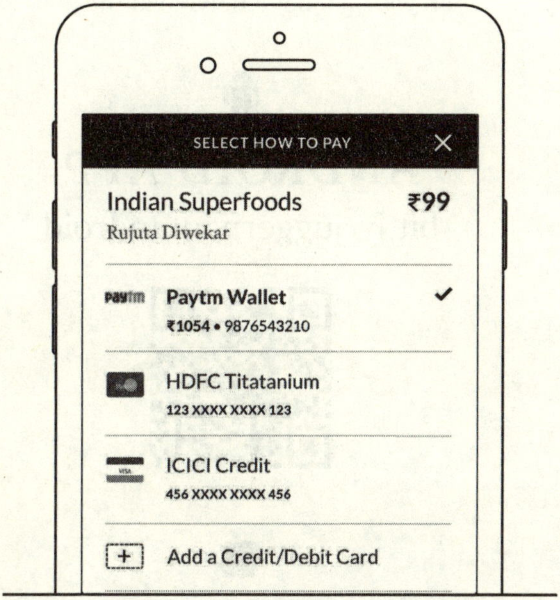


## Paytm Wallet, Cards & Apple Payments

On Android, just add a Paytm Wallet once and buy any book with one tap. On iOS, pay with one tap with your iTunes-linked debit/credit card.

Click the QR Code with a QR scanner app
or type the link into the Internet browser
on your phone to download the app.

## ANDROID APP

bit.ly/juggernautandroid

## iOS APP

bit.ly/juggernautios

For our complete catalogue, visit www.juggernaut.in
To submit your book, send a synopsis and two
sample chapters to books@juggernaut.in
For all other queries, write to contact@juggernaut.in